KEK VERSUS CTHULHU

Edited by Gavin Chappell

Rogue Planet Press

Copyright © 2021 Rogue Planet Press

All rights reserved. Individual stories and artwork are copyright (C) 2021 to the respective authors.

Cover art copyright (C) Toe Keen 2021

The characters and events portrayed in this book are fictitious. Any similarity to real persons, living or dead, is coincidental and not intended by the author.

No part of this book may be reproduced, or stored in a retrieval system, or transmitted in any form or by any means, electronic, mechanical, photocopying, recording, or otherwise, without express written permission of the publisher.

ISBN: 9798701597837

CONTENTS

INTRODUCTION

A god has risen.

An elder god of chaos. A god that the Dark Land of Egypt once knew. A frog headed abomination that dwells—where? in the gloom of the collective unconscious? in the crazy depths of the internet? in the minds of conspiracy theorists and muddle minded political fanatics? As insubstantial as a dream—or a nightmare.

In a world increasingly fragmented, where right and left, atheism and religion, sanity and lunacy struggle for supremacy, who is the true manifestation of *Kek*?

RETURN OF THE KING OF CHAOS

by Norbert Gora

the world stripped of rules
standing at the gates of bloody chaos
bathed its face in the lake of madness
in the ocean of decay

when the first wings of anarchy
soared towards the feathery clouds
he returned unnoticed
the king of eternal chaos

saturated with hatred
burning in human veins like fire
he dipped the globe
in the sea of suffering

mindless masses
fell on their knees
among the ashes of better times
sobs can be heard

the sun's rays

      still stinging watery eyes
      but with the last thought of him
      the charm of dawn will go away into noth-
ingness
      the king of chaos returned
      broke through the barriers of time
      anguish for bodies and souls
      until the end of beating hearts

Norbert Gora is a 27-years old poet and writer from Poland. Many of his horror, SF and romance short stories have been published in his home country. He is also author of many poems in English-language poetry anthologies around the world

THE GOLDEN BOY

Tyson West

In the burst of activity and confusion following his parents dropping him off at his freshman dorm at Miskatonic University, the last thing David expected was a knock on his door from a tall blond upper-class co-ed smiling and calling him by name. "David Lilith?"

He nodded uneasily.

"Hi, I'm Calista Pruitt. I'm with the Young Constitutionalists. We would like to welcome you to Miskatonic University. And is your roommate Tab Bricklin here as well?"

"No. He hasn't arrived yet."

"I'd like to leave these pamphlets for you and Tab." She smiled sweetly. "We realize that the first days here are hectic, and you will have orientation meetings, but the Young Constitutionalists club is very active at Miskatonic. You should make time for us. We meet once a week and we're having a special meeting to welcome all the new freshmen who have a taste for our flavour of politics. We meet at Asteroth Hall auditorium, Thursday of this week at 8:00 p.m. Why don't you tell Tab when he gets here?"

"Tab was supposed to be here yesterday. The first orientation is late this afternoon. Maybe he changed his mind about coming here."

Calista lowered her voice, "At this stage they don't change their mind. Let him know that you are both needed."

She winked seductively, a gesture which seemed strangely out of place in the military precision of her haircut and dark olive woollen suit, with matching green pumps and nylons. David, who had been apolitical in high school, wondered for just an instant at the smile in her eyes, whether she might be interested in him.

"By the way," she murmured, "there will be lots of freshman girls and upper-class co-eds who are looking for the right kind of freshman. You look like you believe in our principles."

"Of cutting taxes and freedom?'

"Absolutely. The only way to kill the beast is by starving it. Government is interfering way too much with real Americans, not to mention bringing in the wrong kind of people into this country." Her tone suddenly turned dark, "Something has got to be done!"

She suddenly flipped her frown. "I'll see you at the meeting. Our group is a great group to hang with."

Calista, in spite of a seemingly frozen helmet of hair, actually flipped her hair just a little as she turned to leave. David was surprised. He didn't think her hair could move at all. He looked at her trim legs and ankles as she turned to knock on the next door.

Maybe he would go to this meeting. It wouldn't hurt to explore what was happening on the campus.

As David put away the last of his tee shirts and socks in the built-in dresser, he turned to see a tall, muscular boy of African-American descent swagger into the room carrying two suitcases. He wore a green shirt covered with check marks, Levi's and sandals. The freshman beanie looked awkward, even silly, on his kinky hair. The stranger grinned and held out his hand to David.

"Are you David, my roommate?"

"Yes. You must be Tab Bricklin."

"You can say that. The instructions I got were a little bit odd. It looks like everybody's pretty much moved in and I'm just getting here."

"Where's your letter?"

"It says that I am supposed to be here no later than tomorrow."

"That's strange. My letter said I was supposed to be here yesterday."

"Must be some kind of a typo."

"Yeah. Our first orientation meeting is this afternoon."

"In that case I better hustle."

Looking at Tab's enormous hands and his light step and his athletic shoes, David decided to venture a guess as to what his activities would be.

"So, are you on the basketball team?"

"Not unless they want to lose all their games. I play the double bass, both in jazz and classical music. That's why they gave me a scholarship."

"I hope you're not going to be practicing here."

"No, no. My stand-up bass is a pretty delicate instrument, I keep it at the music centre, unless of course I'm doing a gig. I play the electric bass as well. I may bring that up here to practice, but I don't plug it into the amp. But mostly, I'll be practicing with a band we're getting together."

"I'll let you get unpacked, we've got a meeting with our hall counsellor in an hour."

"Damn! If I didn't do things ahead of time, I might have missed a lot of these meetings."

"By the way, an upper classman came by, sophomore, real attractive, and gave me a pamphlet and left one for you, about a meeting of the Young Constitutionalists, Thursday."

"That's okay, you can keep mine," he said. "As a black, I'd be about as welcome in the Constitutionalists' Party as Abe Lincoln would have been at a Klan Rally."

David frowned. "They have some black members in the Constitutionalists Party, both congressmen and a senator."

"Yeah, really light skinned tokens and Uncle Toms. Let's not talk politics. Let's just keep it that we're a couple of freshmen together in this brand-new experience called the Miskatonic University and get along. I'll be hanging out with most of my musician buddies. Do you play anything?"

"No, I'll probably join the debate squad. I'm going to explore a bunch of activities to see if there is anything I am interested in."

"Do they have a Chapter of the Young Justinians here?"

"If they have Constitutionalists, they probably have their opponents." David grinned, "I'm kind of hoping to find someplace I can meet girls. The girl that came by with this pamphlet was pretty good looking. I wonder if the rest of them are like that?"

"I'll let you figure that one out on your own," Tab laughed. "Being a musician, I've never had any trouble getting girls."

"Lucky for you."

"Let's go. Before we get girls, we got to get oriented."

David and Tab shook hands. Tab's hand was strong, very strong, but if he was on the liberal side as a musician and doing his own thing, he probably would be a pretty good roommate.

The next week was a swirl of meetings and books ad orientation. David, in taking some of his first classes, realized he had a lot to learn. High school bull sessions and the rumours they spread were not the greatest sources of information as to what college was really like. Economics might be a little drier than he had hoped. History was a lot more interesting.

He had until next week to change his class schedule.

On the evening of the Young Constitutionalists meeting, according to campus tradition, David still had to wear his freshman beanie. He hoped to arrive at this meeting looking cool.

When David slipped into the room, he wasn't sure he was at the right place. The sign in the hallway did say "Young Constitutionalists Meeting." However, many of the students had very short haircuts, and did look somewhat military, like hard core ROTC cadets. Two students with shaved heads in the corner were arguing over who was a purer American. Finally, the lighter skinned of the two reached out and sharply slapped himself in the face. His cheek turned crimson.

"There!" he said, "There's your proof! Blood in the face."

The very slightly olive-skinned, Mediterranean-looking student with broad, powerful shoulders, spoke. "Do what you want. But I'm as much an American as you are." He then struck himself in the face in an identical manner. Although his face reddened slightly, it nowhere matched the red of the other.

David took his seat in the back, wishing he had his roommate with him or someone for support. Then, out of the corner of his eye, he caught two other freshmen and decided to join them. He introduced himself, and they reciprocated but clearly, they appeared as nervous and out-out-place as he was. The three sat silently as they casually glanced around the room. Without any prompting, they finally focused on a bevy of freshmen girls sitting together near the front of the hall.

Sizing up the girls, the boys didn't even notice the tall upper classman who stood up in front of the meeting until his voice boomed, "Welcome all ye Constitutionalists. We are here to save this university and the United States of America from the forces that seek to destroy it."

The fervour of his tone rattled David. As he looked to the front of the hall, he saw the senior with dark, straight hair combed back, dressed like a preppy, catch the attention of the group.

"My name is Brian Dunlevy. I'm a senior and president of the Miskatonic University Young Constitutionalists. We're here to get you all active in politics. We have an enemy greater than the Justinian Party, an enemy greater than the atheists who seek to deny our God and destroy the moral foundation of this country. That enemy is indifference. Only the fervour in our souls to stand up and be willing to die to protect everything near and dear to us will stop this enemy from overwhelming us. The Justinian party is merely one of the pawns our enemies employ to lull us into a sense of false security."

Brian carried on for a good half hour, describing the club in glowing terms, then concluded, "There are a lot of activities on this campus, the pep club, the basket-weaving, music and arts. You only have time to do so much. I'm asking you to strongly consider putting your time, energy and skill into the Young Constitutionalists. We are asking you to believe truly in the sacrifice for change we stand for.

"We have snacks and beer in the next room and would love to mix with and talk to everyone. There will be a sign-up sheet for those of you who want to commit. We need help going door-to-door. We put up signs. We help get out to vote. Our convention later in the year is open to everyone who puts in enough time. Welcome."

As David surmised, the two freshmen next to him came more with the hope of meeting a "hot chick" than joining a political movement. Each of them stood up, put their name on the list, sign-up sheet, and went next door to the mixer. They wandered into the big room, unsure of themselves but drifting toward the freshmen girls. By the end of the evening, Brian met David and each male and female freshman in the room. Brian shook their hands personally and asked them to join. Calista, by Brian's side, encouraged their participation and introduced several of the freshmen boys to the freshmen girls. David smiled as he realized that political organizing was less principle and more a social club competing with another social club to grow a group. In spite of the few very short-haired men whose muscles seemed to be busting out of their green tee shirt uniforms, it seemed all so innocent.

The two other freshmen boys who had been sitting with him had happily paired up with a couple of plump, plain freshmen girls. Although David quite frankly expected the same, he was shocked when Eleanor, a slender, red-headed sophomore, with a shy laugh, and as precise a haircut as Calista's, only shaped a little more naturally, suddenly started showing a great deal of interest in him.

Eleanor's smiles and a couple of beers under his belt left him in a blur of uneasiness and excitement. He left the meeting having made new friends and Eleanor's phone number in his pocket with her strong encouragement to call. The next day, David switched his elective class from economics to political science.

Over the next few weeks, David began attending Young Constitutionalists meetings on a regular basis. Brian and Calista seemed to be paying special attention to him, and to Eleanor. David and Eleanor had developed somewhat of a warming friendship. There had been a bit of handholding and kissing, but Eleanor discouraged anything more physical. As the weeks went by, Brian and

Calista brought David and Eleanor more into the inner circle. David and Eleanor both canvassed for the Constitutionalist candidates and went door-to-door in some of the poor neighbourhoods of Arkham. They were surprised that many of the voters, who answered the door, were less than polite when they explained they were canvassing on behalf of the Constitutionalist candidates. David and Eleanor got through the rough reception by some angry voters and suffering this together brought them closer.

Although the Constitutionalist candidate barely lost the election for congress, at the post-election consolation victory party, Brian and Calista took Eleanor and David aside in a quiet moment. Brian focused his dark brown eyes on the two of them.

"I want to thank the two of you for all your efforts. We think we won significantly more of the 4th Ward because of the efforts you two put into it. We're proud of both of you. Calista and I would like to invite the two of you to a special meeting of the inner circle next week. It's going to be a dinner meeting, so save your Friday night for it. We think the two of you have a lot of potential. David, you could be our golden boy!"

David was even more surprised when he took Eleanor back to her dorm that night. She let him kiss her with a little more passion than she normally encouraged. She still didn't invite him in, but he sensed inertia moving them in that direction.

Despite his political activities, David did well enough in classes to make the Dean's list. For the second semester, he took an additional, the next level, poly sci course.

His roommate, Tab, had numerous girls hanging with him. David and Tab kept their discussions free of politics. They both cheered on the university sports teams and focused on what they had in common.

Although David and Tab were cordial, David did not expect Tab to wave him to come over to his table at the Student Union, where Tab was holding court with a black basketball player and two straight-haired, slender women; one with brown hair to the middle of her back, and the other with shorter shoulder-length hair framing the intense expression on her olive complected face.

When David approached, Tab graciously smiled. "I'd like to introduce you to my good friend Clarence, and our friends Judy Fortran and Catalan Naranja. Catalan is into politics like you, except she's with the Justinian Party." David stiffened up.

Catalan smiled, "It's always wonderful talking to some of our worthy opposition, as long as you're not too far into the darkness of Kek."

"Kek?" David looked bewildered. "What's Kek?"

Catalan grinned. "David, Honey, we'll talk

about this a little bit later." The group lightly chattered on about the school's basketball team with Clarence and what the prospects were for getting into the NCAA tournament. As Tab, Clarence and Judy got up to go to class, Catalan turned to David. "I don't have a class for another hour. When's your next class, Honey?"

"In an hour."

"Well, that may not be enough time for me to tell you about Kek but at least it's a beginning."

As the others trailed off, David sat alone with Catalan, who whispered to him, "You seem like a nice guy and you need to know the truth. A lot of us in the Justinian Party are neopagans. We believe that, call it what you want, God or the Goddess, Allah, Cthulhu or some collective unconscious, is indifferent. God is not some kind of all loving father. We don't believe in evil, except maybe in the hearts of men. God wound up the universe and released it, then God just goes on about God's business. If he helps man out, great, if he doesn't, too bad. How many minorities, blacks and Hispanics or Asians are in the Constitutionalist Party?"

"There's one black and one Asian in our groups."

"Pretty much, Honey, the rest of them are solid white, right?"

"Yes."

"Do any of them wear green shirts or have green arm bands with the letter 'K' on them?"

"Yes, I did see a few, but mostly with guards

that surround Brian and Calista. No, they are like security at a rock concert. We don't want meetings to turn into a mosh pit."

"Honey, they're the green shirts. They're a strong-armed group so if someone gets out of line, they will deal with it. I noticed a freshman went missing last week."

"Yes."

"Yes, but I've noticed a lot of freshmen have dropped out."

"Well, this one dropped out permanently."

"Oh, you mean John Cornin?"

"Yes."

"He was in Bolt Hall, the dorm across from ours. Apparently, he died in a car accident. One shouldn't drink and drive."

"We noticed that anyone Brian doesn't like may end up missing. Rumour has it they thought John was a plant."

"John was a member as I recall but didn't seem to be too active."

"Well they might have been saving him for something. Maybe he figured out he didn't like the agenda. Maybe he knew too much."

"You sound kind of weird and paranoid." David stood up angrily.

"You sit down," Catalan whispered.

In spite of his anger, David sat down.

"The point I'm making with you is they aren't afraid to lose a member once in a while. It may look like an accident, and with young people, society always loses a few of them growing up. Watch out getting too deep into this. You may find it a lot more dangerous than you thought. There is a belief in the followers of Kek, that Kek is absolutely good and absolute evil opposes him. We Justinians may believe in a wishy-washy God, like a Buddhist God, or a neopagan like me who believes in the Goddess, but regardless of how much the Goddess may love me, she won't stop things from happening. Events may happen to our benefit, they may happen against us, but the most we can do is learn from them. There are even a few, who worship Cthulhu. I think it's their inside joke. Cthulhu doesn't hate anyone, he just doesn't want anyone to get in his way. He is like a hurricane that doesn't care where it hits and what damage it does. It's going to go where it wants to go, and it moves beyond good and evil.

"You seem like a nice guy—too nice to really last with the Constitutionalists. The Justinians are at a different end of the spectrum. There's a difference in our approach. We Justinians are pretty disorganized and laid back. We put our agenda forth and hope people vote our ways. We try to persuade people. The Constitutionalists, however, are absolutely obsessed with gaining power at all cost. They will lie, cheat, steal, and even kill to get on top."

"That's it!" David said indignantly as he stood up. "Kill? That absurd."

"Well, think about it, I wouldn't be surprised

if there were more. Do you know what the Horst Wessel song is?"

"What do you mean?"

"It became the unofficial anthem of the Nazi Party in Germany. It was supposedly written by Horst Wessel who was a street thug that fought for the Nazis and died in some brawl in the 1920s. He'd be totally forgotten if he hadn't written that song. I wouldn't have been surprised if the Nazis put him in a place where he was going to get killed. You can't get a really intense movement without a martyr or two. They didn't crucify Christ for nothing. I hope your girlfriend isn't the next Joan of Arc. They did John in, now they need a girl to balance it out. They'll have a great funeral, they will weep and cry for her, and wave her bloody blouse. They always give the animal they are going to sacrifice the best food. It all seems wonderful and great until a knife comes out of nowhere and slits her carotid artery and life bleeds out before your eyes. Kek feeds on blood and darkness. Don't forget it."

A stocky woman, not even 5'2," Catalan, stood up, seeming far taller. "I hope I see you around." She turned, and David watched her wide hips and thick waist. Compared to Eleanor's slender form and graceful motions, Catalan was pathetic.

David stood up and shook his head, thinking, "Some people don't like success in others. Jealously pushes truth aside." Still, as he walked on to his next class, he did recall that some of the Frog-men seemed to share back slaps, and secret signs and code words with one another. Now that he thought about it, they acted a little like a gang. So what, at least he and Eleanor were in good standing with the gang. Although he saw Catalan each week in his English class, and she was cordial, they never discussed the Young Constitutionalists or politics again for that matter.

As winter was coming to an end David learned that the Young Constitutionalists Convention was to be held in late April near Easter during Spring break. Eleanor and David were already excited about getting away to the resort at Chickahominy Beach. Although the old hotel on the ocean had seen better days, it had many spacious meeting rooms and was located near the new Garrison Towers Resort where the State Constitutionalist Convention was being held at the same time. David and Eleanor were both sent out ahead on the Thursday to work with the crew setting up the boiler room supporting the candidate that Brian was backing for State president of the Young Constitutionalists, Bruce Honshell. The Young Constitutionalists Club from Miskatonic's rival university, Arkham University, was backing Louise Abbess for the job.

Before they left, Eleanor, David and Jessie and Frank, a couple of juniors, gathered the computer and communication equipment to set up the boiler room where their side would poll anticipated votes for each candidate ahead of the actual vote.

Brian expected press coverage and worked with the organizers of the State Convention to have lots of his young followers ready for demonstrations and to add an extra cheering section for Senator Cook's speech to the State Convention.

Brian pulled David aside before David left. "I am sending you in early and I will be sending more operatives in tomorrow. I want you to take some of the Frogmen and keep an eye on things. I am especially concerned about the protesters. They will do anything they can to disrupt Senator Cook's speech and give him a black eye. We want to be sure that Bruce wins as State Chairman of the Young Constitutionalists, and we also want to be sure that the convention re-nominates Senator Cook without dissention, although his nomination is pretty much a foregone conclusion. The state-wide race against Governor Clark in November is not. Senator Cook called for a border wall and other solutions to keep the less desirables out of our country. If we do not keep the evil out, it will flow in and overwhelm us. You and Eleanor need to learn and also help as much as you can. You've never been to a convention before, have you?"

"No."

"You need to learn the importance of innuendo, spreading negative information, and keeping your eye on the enemy. The enemy is cagy and adaptable." David was taken aback. Brian bore his brown eyes into David's soul. "I can tell you are concerned about negative information. I believe you think we might even be out of line—perhaps if we were in a perfect world. As long as evil exists, the world cannot be perfect. Perhaps the truth is a fluid thing and we don't necessarily know what it may be from time-to-time. Forces of darkness are going to overcome this country. If we don't employ some darkness to fight the darkness, we will never come into the light. You and Eleanor are showing a lot of promise as Young Constitutionalists. Who knows, maybe someday you will be running for office yourself. I will be proud to support you when you have matured."

Eleanor had on a spaghetti-strap blouse and tight jeans. "The two of you have a bright future together." Brian put one hand on David's shoulder and held Eleanor's hand with his other. "It means a lot to me to be bringing you along as such a powerful couple." Eleanor looked at David with a warm glow.

As David and Eleanor slid in the back seat with another worker, David reached out and grabbed Eleanor's hand, "I didn't know we were a couple."

She smiled, "Neither did I, but I guess it's something that happens naturally."

"They want us to work with the Frogmen down there to make sure security's tight, I guess we need to tag along and learn as much as we can."

She reached over and put her arm around him and hugged him. "David, you're wonderful."

David felt a chill of worry. He thought of Catalan's words. He did not want to lose Eleanor.

When they got to the hotel, David worked with the crew setting up the computer system in the boiler room. Each of them with their cell phones would be calling in tips and information to Central. Central would organize the information and Calista was there to coordinate sending bright young operators to try to persuade the less committed to vote with them. Calista met with several enthusiastic followers who began spreading false rumours that Louise was a secret agent of the Justinian Party and that she had sub-Saharan African blood in her, and that her husband was a felon.

Delegates of all kinds and shapes began arriving in town from all over the state to hear Senator Cook's long anticipated address. Sure enough, a huge crowd of protesters, peppered with minorities and members of the Justinian Party, gathered across the street. David looked over at the ominous crowd singing and chanting. He was not shocked to see Catalan was carrying a sign that showed a boiling pot and the slogan, "We need to stop cooking racism."

The Constitutionalist security detail, mostly Frogmen, with green armbands, formed up at the gate to protect all the arriving delegates. As they waited for Brian and Calista, David turned to

Eleanor. "How long will this protest go on? Seems like it's gone on for a couple hours so far."

Eleanor shook her head. "Rumour has it, it may go on through tomorrow."

"I can't believe these people are so much against freedom and individual responsibility."

"Neither can I," David demurred.

A limo pulled up and Brian and Calista got out. Not missing a beat before he entered, Brian paused and went up to David and shook his hand. "It's good to see you're here. I've been hearing good reports on you."

David was shocked Brian would even notice him in this big mass of humanity.

David stammered, "Thank you, Sir. I'm doing my best."

"I appreciate that," Brian responded, and patted him on the back.

That night, things between David and Eleanor got even more intimate. She and he had a couple glasses of wine with dinner, and amid the hubbub, she invited him to her room. There, they began making out, and one thing led to another. Eleanor held him and whispered quietly, "I love you."

David in a soft, sincere voice spoke, "I love you, Eleanor. It seems every good thing I have has come through the Constitutionalist Party."

"Just about everything." Eleanor giggled. "When you arrived on campus, you were just a little dweeb from a small town. You've come a long way.

"Why don't you wear your light tan suit tomorrow," she added, "you look good in it."

"Okay, darling, whatever you say." David felt she was already getting possessive of him and his looks just like a good wife would. It made him feel secure.

"My roommate's coming back in a little while. We'd better get up and get dressed."

"I just want to spend the whole night with you."

"That's something we can always look forward to."

The next day before breakfast, Brian called both of them to meet with him in the boiler room. Brian had decided to organize a counter-demonstration. "David, you and Eleanor will lead it. We have signs and the Frogmen will set up a security perimeter. We're afraid they might try to come and get us or do some violence. David, I'll talk with Kurt, the leader of Frogmen. They planned to come in the opposite direction and stay on the east side of the street while the protesters were on the west side. We'll be having a lot of Frogmen scattered among the group of protesters, to protect us. These Justinians preach nonviolence but it is part of their hypocrisy. They and their Cthulhu are out for blood."

David and Eleanor arrived at the parking lot, which was the staging area for the counter-protest. There were bundles of pre-made green signs with Constitutionalist slogans. A crowd was gathering in the parking lot to the north with quite a few burley men who looked a lot older than the students, even though most of their signs had on them phrases such as "Students for Democracy, Students for Freedom or Students for Justice."

"Okay," Kurt said. "David, you grab that sign, Eleanor you grab that one, and the two of you carry a sign."

David didn't even look at his sign but grabbed it and held the stick to hold it above his head. Eleanor grabbed hers, the demonstrators fell behind them in order, and marched down the sidewalk. David made sure to walk between Eleanor and the protestors. In case they threw rocks, he wanted to be able to shield Eleanor.

On the other side, the Justinians were locking arms and singing, "We Shall Overcome," and stayed on their side of the street.

Suddenly, David began chanting, "2-4-6-8 We Don't Want This Country to Disintegrate," and then other Constitutionalists took up the chant and added, "No Foreigners, No Foreigners, No Terrorists, No Terrorists." David worked to keep his crowd separate from the other group. Suddenly, David was shocked to see that some older men in his group started pushing his crowd out toward the centre of the street. On the other side, wearing cut-offs, were similar-looking older men in the Justinian Group, who started pushing their crowd out toward the centre of the street.

Checking to be sure Eleanor was close, David yelled, "No. We stay on this side of the street. No violence."

Suddenly, a car came barrelling down the street, not stopping in spite of the crowd.

David, as he stood on the edge of the curve crying for his group to get back onto the sidewalk, felt a shove against his back.

He turned to see Eleanor had pushed him in front of the speeding car. The car struck.

He looked up from the pavement in pain to see Tab Bricklin, his roommate at the dorm, grinning behind the wheel. Tab threw the car into reverse and barrelled away. No one tried to stop him. Eleanor was over him. "Darling, what's the matter? Are you all right?" she screamed. "They're murdering my boyfriend. They murdered my boyfriend."

Suddenly the thuggish-looking demonstrators, and a phalanx that had stayed hidden until now, on the Constitutionalist side, began pummelling the Justinian demonstrators. David, though injured and in pain, looked up and noticed suddenly that the demonstrators that appeared to be part of the Justinian group, were in fact herding the Justinian demonstrators toward the Frogmen on the Constitutionalist side.

A cry had gone up, "They murdered David. A minority murdered one of our own."

A full-scale riot broke out. David lay there

bleeding. Although Eleanor was above him and holding him, she did not try to stop the bleeding or call for help.

She turned to David as he lay there about ready to pass out. "Your tan suit makes great photos of your blood, that's why I had you wear it. I want to let you know I'll never forget you, David. You had such a bright future, it's too bad, but unless the chosen one dies, it isn't real. I loved you, Golden Boy." She kissed him as his eyes closed, and stood up and screamed, "They've killed him! They've murdered him! Those Cthulhu-worshiping monsters have killed my fiancé!"

Tyson West lives in Eastern Washington in smoke and dust on the bottom of an Ice Age flood plain. He enjoys reciting his poetry to magpies and coyotes.

He has published poetry and speculative fiction in various genres in "Fast Forward Festival", Voluted Tales, and in anthologies "Warlords of the Asteroid Belt", and "You Can't Kill Me I'm Already Dead". He has had two poems nominated for the Pushcart Prize. His poetry collection "Home-Canned Forbidden Fruit" is available from Gribble Press. He received third place in the 2nd Annual Kalanithi Contest for his rondel "Under the Bridge".

For more information please see his profile on "Haiku Registry" online.

HYPNOTOAD

Mathias Jansson

Without thinking
we all shared that funny gif
with the hypnotic toad
from Futurama
to our friends

His mesmerising eyes
made us laugh
we spread his image
in social media
like a plague

We joined the fake religion
of Kek at 4chan
worshipped Pepe the frog
and ended all our comments
with a praise Kek
because it was so funny

But when our friends
and family started to change
moving around like zombies
mumbling praise Kek
and chaos spread in the world

we realised something was wrong

We went off the grid
to protect ourselves
started to analyse the gif
frame by frame
and found subliminal messages
ancient spells from the Old Kingdom
summoning the Ogdoad
from their exile
in the eternal darkness

As we stared at the animation
in our handmade flip book
we suddenly realized
we had done wrong all the time
who doesn't love
a funny hypnotoad?
Praise Kek!

Mathias Jansson is a Swedish art critic and horror poet. He has been published in magazines as The Horror Zine, Dark Eclipse, Schlock and The Sirens Call. He has also contributed to over 100 different horror anthologies from publishers as Horrified Press, James Ward Kirk Fiction, Source Point Press, Thirteen Press etc. Homepage: http://mathiasjansson72.blogspot.se/ Amazon author page: http://www.amazon.co.uk/Mathias-Jansson/e/B00BTDBYBQ/ref=sr_ntt_srch_lnk_4? qid=1366806658&sr=8-4

DARKNESS ASCENDING

by Sergio 'ente per ente' PALUMBO
edited by Michele DUTCHER

Joan Martínez's blue eyes looked outside the window. The sky above promised that the remainder of the late evening and the incoming night could only grow warmer. After all, it was summer and could not be different.

Though something else would be soon different, very different, he told himself. It would change everything, he was certain about it. *The young man knew it…*

Those usual words of the ritual came to his mind, again. *Kekuit be blessed, Kekuit come!* How could things be otherwise?

He touched his short dark hair that barely reached the nape of his neck. The curls in the middle looked more shapeless than yesterday, but he didn't make any attempt to tidy them. His small home was situated near the coast and the Mediterranean Sea could be easily spotted outside, in the distance, if you just focused your eyes far enough ahead. Though what lay in the streets of the neighbourhood he lived in and on the beaches that were available all around wasn't particularly of interest to him.

La Barceloneta, constructed during the 17th and 18th centuries, was roughly triangular, bordered by the sea, originally filled only with a very few residents who took part in activities of the small port. Continuing to be perceived as foreign to the larger city where it was located, because of the architecture and the food, it looked like a neighbourhood with vibrancy and soul. This was in spite of the fact that many thought it was, at least to tourists, no more than a sort of theme park that reached its maximum entertainment level only on hot summer days like this.

Nowadays, the locals were complaining about everything from noise and litter to rising prices, as most of them could only afford to drink and eat day by day a small glass of beer from a barrel and the most typical of the *tapas* called the 'bomba', which was a ball of potatoes filled with meat and the selection of spicy sauce, and nothing else.

Over the past several years the quality of the sand itself on the beaches had become a source of continued controversy. Once, the main entrancement of this area had been getting lost in the side streets or alleyways, next to markets, small nightclubs and restaurants. However, today this might turn into a very bad mistake, given the number of murderous delinquents you could run into by chance at night here and there, looking for wealthy people from abroad with lots of money that could be stolen by force. Other than that, the yellow line, which was the metro line that stopped here, was the most popular for pickpocketing...

There were too many problems nowadays—actually it had been so for many long years—that imposed a heavy burden on an already strained economy. Joan was still a youngster when everything, from the government to the conditions of the people itself, had begun to collapse, but he still remembered it all very well. This was also the reason why he had gone abroad, of course, after graduating, many years ago, in search of better chances of a good career. After all, there were not many possibilities to get a good job in that part of Spain, and it had been that way for a very long time, Joan was well aware of it. The bad economy during that period wasn't really that different from Greece's. *But at least the Greeks had ancient monuments, world-renowned temples and great tourist attractions that the present Catalonia certainly didn't possess...* From many points of view, this neighbourhood was lacking significant links to the past—even with its churches, in the centre of the neighbourhood itself, there was only the History Museum of Catalonia. There was also a small museum, called 'Casa de la Barceloneta', which was housed in a preserved building dating back to 1761 with letters and number engraved that were inscriptions of the plots used in construction.

Perhaps a third of the visitors to this place arrived on a large boat, but they didn't stay in hotels, didn't stop for long and very frequently didn't even eat in local restaurants. There had once also been an aquarium, where one could discover the great quantity of marine life of the Mediterranean Sea, though it had long fallen into disuse because of the economic downturn, and the building appeared to be in very bad condition now.

All of that was the first reason why Joan had been forced to go abroad, the same as many young people all over southern Europe at that time, to advance their studies and to find better jobs. Undoubtedly, he had found his way, truth be told, and after completing his academic course, it had also been a great opportunity to become a young researcher at LHC, the world's largest and most powerful particle accelerator that was situated just inside the famous laboratory, built between the border of France and Switzerland, near Geneva.

But the move had cost him dearly, especially because nothing was easily granted to young, foreign researchers, especially when they couldn't show they had already achieved renown thanks to being published or having their innovations tested in the field somewhere before. That was something Joan didn't have at that time, of course. He could have never achieved such renown in his tiny hometown in Spain.

But he had worked hard. He had his own reasons to do so... Obviously, Geneva labs were an important site for research and not everyone gained access there. But he had made it, in the end!

It was there, in those labs built under the ground surface, that many physicists and engineers were probing the fundamental structure of universal matter. And it was down there that a 27-year-old Joan Martínez had been able to lay his eyes on, and have a first-hand read of, the reports on the theories of computer quantum viruses that only a few scientists were trying to presuppose at that time and, possibly, further elaborate later on. And he had taken a full advantage of everything he read and saw, which had also deeply changed his life. What he had seen was going to change everything in the world soon, if he just proved capable of accomplishing his task, which might have been relegated into the world of dreams before such studies had become part of his knowledge, for sure.

Truth be told, over the course of the next five years he hadn't only become a very capable researcher in the field of physics. He had achieved abundant experience in the field of computers, and the subtleties of the web, which was what he had also intelligently, and always, relied on. He did share his goals and hidden ends, with others who thought exactly like him about the world. They didn't make use of the common means of communication, certainly. There were other safer, more secretive and useful ways to correspond...

The deep web, also called hidden web, which was that part of the World Wide Web whose contents were not indexed by standard search engines, had first been called this in 2000 after the definition given by a computer scientist. Certainly, it had been operating long before it was openly recognized worldwide. It also had another smaller portion called the dark web that was usually inaccessible through common methods and was apparently invisible, different from the surface web most internet users knew and made use of day by day. Provided that the majority of the information kept there was well hidden or locked inside databases, and not for the eyes of most of the people, a lot of illegal activities or disreputable actions had been planned or even perpetrated through it. This was exactly what Joan's group had made use of for their purposes, by using a specially-designed software that allowed them to get to the contents intentionally hidden from the regular internet for making their purposes come true.

Now it was time for the darkest, and deadliest of

all researches, possibly. Why, you could ask at this point. And the reply was something known only to Joan and his group of same-minded persons. *'Because we're in the business of bringing Kekuit, the old deity, back into the world that had almost entirely forgotten her, that's why!'* the young man told himself wide-eyed and smiled.

Madmen, this was what some people would call them, he knew it. *Kekuit be blessed, Kekuit come!* This was all that really mattered...

Quantum physics, Joan's preferred field of research, was largely an unknown science to the common citizen. Surprisingly, it could be simple to sum it up, even though understanding it thoroughly was considerably more difficult. As a matter of fact, quantum physics was interested in the behaviour of photons and the various invisible particles, and it contrasted with classical physics, which was about the behaviour of everyday objects that were large enough to see.

In a way, the main difference between classical physics and quantum science was really very weird given the fact that the objects that we can watch in the world around us behave in a way that seems intuitive, but once we start to consider very small objects, intuition and common sense have to be abandoned... Instead, when we consider them individually, photons and other particles behave in a way that most people would be ready to depict as implausible.

Perhaps one of the most unbelievable things

that can happen in the realm of the invisible, if you want to call it that, was that objects such as photons can be in two places at the same time or in two different states at once—a so-called state of *superposition*. And scientists had confirmed that this peculiar behaviour really did happen, despite indications to the contrary whenever we tried to directly look at it. Another strange effect was called *quantum mechanical tunnelling*, which referred to the fact that a tiny object was capable of passing straight through a barrier without damaging it. So, for example, if you fired a particle against an obstacle, there was a possibility that it could appear on the other side with the obstacle itself still intact. In reality, photons had the properties of both particles and waves, or, in other words, both images were correct!

Wave theory was all about probability. In other words, it was the probability of a particle being at any particular point in space and, until it was directly seen, its position could be thought of as all points in space, albeit with some places being more likely than others. Quantum entanglement occurred when pairs or groups of particles were generated, or interacted in ways such that the quantum state of each particle couldn't be indicated independently from the others: even when the particles were separated by a large distance—instead, a quantum state had been taken for the system as a whole.

Theories of Quantum Viruses were originated from exactly such science... Though, it was much more complicated than could be said in just a few words, of course!

Since the young man had laid his eyes on that piece of research about the theories of computer quantum viruses, he had known it could be done, in reality. *It had to be done, actually!* But he—and the few others who followed the same old beliefs as he—had to work really hard for that goal to be reached...

Kekuit be blessed, Kekuit come!

Joan looked at the watch at his wrist and saw it was almost time. So, he headed for his computer where his seat stood. He was always connected, of course, but the particular window for his secretive and important communication would open soon.

So, why were they trying to insert quantum viruses and not an empowered modern, although unbelievably efficacious, computer virus for their hidden ends, whatever they were? If you thought of a code that was totally indestructible, experience reported that however sophisticated it might be, all it took was a sufficiently powerful computer and encrypted messages could be accessed. Not so with quantum cryptography... This wasn't a code that was so difficult that it would take all the computers on the planet years to crack. According to the laws of quantum physics, a quantum virus that had its data protected by means of such a method of encryption was totally secure!

Everything came from the subtleties of quantum measurement, Joan considered. In quantum physics, a single measurement could give you the answer to thousands, perhaps millions, of calculations done in parallel by quantum particles, and quantum cryptography protected information in an unprecedented way. Such a new technology and its great possibilities obviously had attracted the attention of governments and industries keen to possess the best machines— and to prevent them falling into the wrong hands. Though, in this case, who had developed that unbelievable result coming out of quantum science was just not some known companies, but him and his group, *that was what people or policemen could consider the most dangerous hands of all.*

Kekuit be blessed, Kekuit come!

Joan was getting more excited as the right time approached. It was only fifteen minutes and then everything would have been finally put into motion. And it would be done!

The young man sat. His computer was endowed with four monitors, five CPUs, countless expansion cards for video and graphics other than many reliable power supply units—. Moreover, everyone in their group had a vast knowledge of application, programming and system software.

Joan considered briefly that, from the Web users' point of view, the links were provided by the system. For example, when someone else's e-mail arrived on your screen, you could, if you wished to do so, edit it—add to it, subtract from it, or change it in some way. This wasn't possible with the copy of the page which arrived on your computer from the server. As a Web user, only three courses of action were usually available: the initial choice of a particular site address; scrolling through a document once you had accessed it; and cutting and pasting from it. The readers, or users, couldn't alter a Web site itself: only the site owner would be capable of doing that. But now, the *quantum viruses* they had secretly developed and tested, could do the same thing, *without any permission*! The types currently released from their group and updated as of today were unable to have complete control over all the sites, but the disruptions, problems and disconnections they gave rise to were really destructive and took place as a deadly shot most of the times!

After all, the visions the Web's inventors had for the internet itself was to have anything being potentially connected with anything else, which was true in the majority of cases nowadays. And their new powerful quantum viruses could make the most of it all and could also spread or cause damages everywhere, regardless of types of network and security solutions put in action or defensive procedures used.

Kekuit be blessed, Kekuit come!

Before the right moment came, Joan's blue

eyes looked around briefly, without saying anything. All of his house was endowed with colourful hieroglyphic writing, an ancient group of a thousand signs and letters used to make words by the ancient Egyptians in the past long gone. They were on the walls, on the cabinets, even on the floor of a few rooms. As active knowledge of such language, that was obviously quite labour-intensive, had long disappeared over the course of the previous centuries, a lot of attempts were made to understand the hidden meaning of the inscriptions and it was only in the 1800s that scholars had begun being able to read them again. Though the term 'hieroglyphics' was a Greek word, the old Egyptians referred to their writing as 'the god's words' and they also believed that those words came from the deities themselves giving humans their system to express their opinions, traditions and way of life.

The meaning of such words, at first, was connected to the briefest notations designed to identify a person or a place and an event. The ancient Egyptians believed that it was important to record and communicate information about religion and government. Most likely the earliest purpose such writing served in human history was in trade, to give information about goods, prices, between one point and another, though the first actual evidences of Egyptian writing directly came from tombs.

People used symbols, pictures to represent

something whenever they needed it, though the problem with pictograms like those was that the information they contained was not much. One might draw a picture of a woman and a temple and a sheep but there was no way of relaying their connection. For example, *was the woman depicted on the right coming from or going to the temple? And was the sheep an offering she was leading to the priests or a gift to her from the priests?* Only archaeologists, or a few learned people, could read and understand those symbols, and Joan Martínez was one of them, of course… Everyone in his group certainly could do so. Other than that, he also knew that all the scripts could easily be read by recognizing the direction the phonograms were facing. Images in any inscription always faced the beginning of the line of text; if the text was to be read left-to-right then the faces of the people, birds, and animals would be looking to the left.

Many would say that covering the walls of a house with such things—visually being more or less figurative, as they represented elements that were at times stylized and simplified, but all generally perfectly recognizable in form—was a sort of strange obsession, *but it wasn't only that.* This was especially true if you were well learned in such a field of ancient knowledge and could recognize at first sight the head of a serpent surmounted by a disk that appeared in the corners of the rooms.

Kekuit be blessed, Kekuit come! He repeated the

phrase in his mind another time.

The moment for the communication via the dark web came, and the window opened on his monitor. Another face, from the other side of the webcam, appeared. It was Aytekin. Dark-haired, with his two deep, strange eyes, he was just two years older than the Spanish researcher, though his features were less pleasing, and harsher.

"How long do you think it will be before we can have our beliefs restored and our dreams come true?" his Turkish friend asked from the other side of the Mediterranean, by means of that social network of theirs. "How long before we can feel the winds of power on our skin?"

"Soon, very soon…" the Spanish man replied, turning his eyes to the webcam and glancing at the traits of Aytekin who sat in his room, on the other side of the expanse of the sea, before his computer with a rapt expression. He happened to see the glimpse of a sort of smile dropping out of the other's lips as he said that. There were a few others like the two of them, situated in Russia, Moldavia, Egypt and other countries in the Middle East, for example, who were waiting, all over the world, after having worked so hard, after so many experiments. "It will only be a matter of minutes before we can start seeing the first signs of what we planned. The first result will be an increasing weakness of the secondary web sites targeted."

"And there be darkness, certainly!" the Turkish young man replied. "And then?"

"There will be hospitals without electricity, power plants without energy, transportation without control. That will be the terrifying experience for the common people who could never expect it to happen one day," the other added. "The beginning of the deep destruction of the present way of life, of the world we had been forced to live in until today..." They stared at each other.

"I simply can't wait, the same as the others!" a very pleased Aytekin uttered. *"Kekuit be blessed, Kekuit come!"*

Joan sneered and nodded while repeating, *"Kekuit be blessed, Kekuit come!* We'll be in touch later by other means, as previously agreed. We can all see it happen!" The communication window closed. The Spanish man thought, silently, that what probably most displeased the ones in their group was that they could not add to the whole world population's grief by confessing that they were the instrument of the world's oncoming desperation, and of their condition to come. In fact, a large number of the people would be already dead because of the destruction their quantum viruses had caused throughout the web, shutting down industries, transportation, security systems and army weaponry. The rest who were still living—and there would be many left on the planet—would soon need to be subjected forcibly to the rules of their deep worship, and would also need to have the religious principles of their deity that had been long lost, and almost forgotten.

Whoever didn't comply with it all, would soon be added to the suffering and death of the millions who had already gone before them, of course.

And no one could ever stop their actions on time. It was too late! *Kekuit be blessed, Kekuit come!*

There were companies that offered services to the police of some countries to get to the bottom of some concealed parts of the dark web itself or for having some structured data extracted from result pages—But his group knew a thing or two about looking after itself. All of them knew very well how to make use of the most common hacking techniques that relied on Keylogger-like software, that recorded the key sequence and strokes of keyboard into a file, or also on Denial-of-Service attacks to briefly take down a site or server by sending a lot of data it was simply not able to deal with. There were also the powerful Eavesdropping, or passive attacks, that allowed hackers like them to easily take control of the computer systems to gain some information without being identified, or the so-called Bait and switch that started running a malicious program elsewhere and allowed a hacker to get unprivileged use of other people's computers.

Phishing had been the main way Joan's group had turned to so they could get money for their purposes during those years of preparation. 'It had been easy, hadn't it?' he thought.

He and his skilful companions had been able to stop all of those dangerous companies or get rid of them once and for all, attacking anyone trying to find out what they were doing, although no one imagined that their actions were behind their demise. One of these, from Japan, probably the most capable and insidious, had been run out of business two years ago, when their efforts to reach some sites his group had created had become too efficient and too efficacious. So, they had made their move before it was too late, and the target of their counter-activities had finally retired… Now the web was less dangerous to their disastrous purposes, and certainly weaker, exactly as they wanted it to be.

Since then, things had become much easier. The most noteworthy thing of all was that they hadn't accomplished their task by turning to some individual resources or secret funding. On the contrary, they had made a good use of their capabilities, their skills and clever minds, and that had proved to be enough once combined together, across the world. There were not many of them, it was true, but just think of what the most intelligent scientists in the field of physics could have done in the past if they had just worked together in complete secrecy, for their own good. Probably they weren't like such most intelligent researchers and academicians in the world, but they didn't necessarily to be. What they had devised, and brought to life, was just enough to achieve their purposes… and for the higher interest of restoring their ancient religious beliefs.

They had turned to the most obscure recesses of the dark web and made it become a lifeless place, meant to be the first step for the rebirth of their old beloved deity called Kekuit. All of their efforts, the quantum viruses' releases were not intended to take control of the internet, there was no Skynet-like robotic attack on the way, as depicted in movies of the past. *They only had the purpose of spreading damages everywhere and finally shutting down the entire web, once and for all.* And this was also going to be the end of the evil and stupid worshippers of Cthulhu itself, who had long put their faith over the internet to spread their purposes, to plan their actions and more easily communicate among themselves, staying away from the eyes of the common citizens, being unbeknownst to everyone or in accordance with some corrupted governments that helped them.

After all, *wasn't it all about the supremacy of one ancient belief over all the others?* Apart from all the religions—they were not the true fighters on battleground, they had never truly been...— there was only that old, secret confrontation, the struggle between the few remaining followers of the Egyptian deity, Kekuit, *may she be blessed,* that almost nobody remembered today, and the ones who wanted to please Cthulhu and had long be waiting for him and his many otherworldly monstrous gods to return to Earth. It had lasted for so many centuries, and most of the world citizens didn't even know about that secret battle...

Kekuit be blessed, Kekuit come! And, since she was finally back, she would never give way to other deities... Joan seemed rather pleased with himself.

This was all because the moment the web itself was dead would also become the point from which their very ancient deity that represented darkness in the ancient myths would rise again as the Bringer-in of the night and cover the whole world under her bulky shadowy presence. *After all, hadn't the world itself taken shape from a dark, endless sea as the oldest myths indicated?* There would no longer be a means for the followers of Cthulhu to act worldwide, and there would no more online resources for all the many worshippers of such unutterable divinities once and for all. But, in doing so, they were also turning internet into a place empty of the many things other believers—*differently from him, and contrary to Kekuit, the old female supreme being...*—most needed to live, with confidence, power and control being the most obvious.

People would die and be injured in disasters all around the world, and that meant not only on the web. Just think of a hospital relying on a computerized control room which immediately became inoperative forever, or a huge transportation system by rail that would collapse after the Big Iron, that was the structures of mainframes themselves, had been deeply damaged and turned into heaps of destroyed CPUs not capable of working anymore. But none of that mattered now, only the result they had in their mind was important. The many deaths and much suffering that would come about as a consequence was an outcome they had already accepted. After all, it was the others who were going to die, not the ones like them, not Joan's group of serious followers of unbelievably powerful Kekuit who had planned it all and would deeply rejoice the cause of their bloody actions.

"Beautiful isn't it?" Joan Martinez found himself asking, though there was no one else around that could hear him undoubtedly. It was just a pleasing consideration that made its way into his mind at present.

Madmen, this was how some people would call them, *hadn't he already said that?* Or also bloody assassins... The young man smiled, as he and his fellows really didn't care. Their ends were certainly superior, the same as their belief was...

As the moment of final victory was now quickly approaching and the destructive quantum viruses released were presently doing their damages, the young man felt a very light wind against his neck coming from outside. Night had already descended upon that neighbourhood. About time... Yes, dawn would come, the sun would rise again, but it would be a very different day, without electricity, modern communications and services. And then, a very deep darkness, the real darkness would descend...Actually, this was going to be the darkest night of all, after so many centuries!

Kekuit be blessed, Kekuit come! Let her blackness wrap the whole world in it again!

All they had devised was now at work allowing it to happen...

It was funny to think that everything had started from a research pertaining to certain features of viruses dimensioned for trying to increase the efficiency of photosynthetic energy transport via quantum effects. And quantum viruses genetically engineered for optimal exciton transport had been created in the end. Being excitons, some neutral quasi-particles consisting of an electron and an electron hole bound together they could transport energy without transporting net charge. The wavelike nature of the particle provided a mechanism for it to simultaneously explore multiple pathways and ultimately resolve the optimal route. As a matter of fact, nature tended to drive quantum systems to the degree of quantum coherence that is 'just right' for attaining maximum efficiency.

What did all this have to do with computer viruses, anyway? Although those viruses had demonstrated the ability to have light energy captured and transferred, the reality had long been that there was no actual reaction centre in the works. Without localized machinery meant to have this energy transduced, there was no way to harness it to produce actual power. Nor was there a mechanism to direct that energy into fuel. At least, this had been so until those exciting new theories in quantum biology had been applied for real.

Having been ascertained that quantum viruses suffered from quantum de-localization, every virus doubled its uncertainty in position after a few minutes. It also followed the principles of quantum physics just like a sub atomic-particle.

On the other hand, in the weird world of quantum computing, the state of computer systems networked together was so fragile that a real access to a single quantum bit on just one machine would require a network-wide reset. There were defences that used some ways to protect the mainframes, like sending out only messages at prearranged intervals, having long average wait times between legitimate network connections, and filled all the unused network time with decoy transmissions. By spreading out network connections over random intervals in time, mainly, some researchers had shown quantum computer scientists could reduce the chance of a successful attack but still kept the performance advantages promised by quantum computing. But this method was not useful against any threat beside malware, because it was inefficient...

It was strange to think that, while quantum computers were only taking their first toddler steps in the world of computer science at that time, the research data the young Spanish man had once come into touch with by chance in those labs had allowed him, and the fellow members of his group, to create and upgrade some real quantum viruses that could easily damage and destroy all the databases present on the web, by making use of their quantum peculiarities to enter or exit at will the most protected sites, virtually being untrackable as they simply left no traces. Other than that, the same rules of quantum mechanics made possible that light particles were linked over a distance through the quantum mechanical property of entanglement to transmit key information in a way that any eavesdropping could be prevented from being detected.

He had not developed such quantum viruses by himself alone—*how could he, anyway?* —although he had stolen the data of the finds made about it and all the reports the theories about such things relied on. That had been the start of their dream!

Kekuit be blessed, Kekuit come!

In creating and perfecting their quantum viruses, they had gone past that old type of malicious software program called 'malware' that, when executed, replicated by reproducing itself or infecting other computer programs by modifying them from the inside. Though, as their new powerful viruses were based upon quantum science rules, they operated on an entirely unprecedented level of effectiveness, proving capable of breaking the encryption of every computer system in the world, and he really meant it! And, once launched, everything was automated, progressing and spreading further on without human intervention. In a few words, it made use of the weak points present in mainframes and went through them by opening quantum backdoors, thus making unattainable for everyone tracking down the origins of the spreading through the whole web.

Kekuit be blessed, Kekuit come! It was a matter of minutes, and what they wanted would become real…

All at once, Joan was briefly distracted by something behind him. Growling angrily, he thought that he didn't have much of a head for any other thing at that moment. Though, the shocking impression he got when he turned his back was unbelievable! He was abruptly silenced…

Something suddenly dashed out of the dimness of the opposite wall of the room, and revealed itself to be a brilliant light that quickly became higher and stronger. *What the hell was it…?*

The light didn't provide him with a clear view of what would happen next. Wordlessly the Spanish man stood, afraid and completely incapable of doing anything, as the flaming thing got nearer and nearer until the warmth was near him and also all around his desk.

The whispers he heard, or better the sort of voice, belonged to the flaming thing that became bigger and bigger, until it began turning itself into a creature! It moved forwards as if it had just crossed an invisible portal from another world. Then it just stood before him and looked at his body in a terrible way.

Wake up! This is just a very bad dream… he told himself. But the presence of the terrifying creature made it clear it wasn't, in reality… He also understood that he wasn't in complete control of his body at the moment, not anymore.

"You… are the mind… behind this… You… you are one of the humans," the voice cried out, "one of the few who planned on… bringing Kekuit to life again… and her darkness!"

Joan's eyes were terrified, there was nothing he could say, nothing he could think of but being overwhelmed by such a flaming presence. He would have said yes, that it had been him and a few others, who had made it possible. However, he simply couldn't speak at all.

"In doing so… you wanted to restore Kekuit's realm on Earth… and you wanted her darkness to wrap everything in it, people, things and the world itself…" the words coming from the creature continued, angry and coarse. They sounded very ancient, slow and heavy, full of power and meaning.

The young man would partly reply, if his voice could come out, but there was no way he could overcome his sense of inferiority.

"In doing so… you also wanted Kekuit to rule from this moment on… forever… over this world.

But you forgot about me! You forgot about Keku!" There was resentment from the presence now, it could be clearly felt.

"What...? The..." but the Spanish man was unable to say anything else, forcibly stopped by his deeper and deeper fear.

"I am Keku, the god of the hour... before dawn. Bringer of the light. And husband of Kekuit! You really forgot about me! I and Kekuit... are both the primordial elements... bringing one also implies bringing the other. And none of us might rule definitely over the other... it has always been so, and it has to be this way also today! There can't be darkness that defeats... the light completely... and there is no light that doesn't come out of darkness..."

There were no more words after those. The creature simply stretched its arms towards the young man and the flames that enveloped the whole surface of its body came with them. Then, the fire was everywhere, on Joan's body too, and his cries of pain began to fill the whole room. Such strong flames appeared to be so powerful and energized that they might very easily destroy the invisible matter the air was made of, and everything else on Earth, so that the place was soon burnt to ashes.

And then all of Joan Martinez's hopes, his worries and thoughts were finally over. This was the same as had happened to the poor unaware people his actions had caused during the previous bloody and unexpected demise all over the world.

Because he had forgotten that important lesson: the dance between the dark and light was always meant to remain, as the night was what allowed us all to see the stars. There was no light without darkness, and also in the deepest blackness there might be a light...

'Sergio is an Italian public servant who graduated from Law School working in the public real estate branch. He has published a Fantasy RolePlaying illustrated Manual, WarBlades, of more than 700 pages. Some of his works and short- stories have been published on American Aphelion Webzine, WeirdYear Webzine, Cheapjack Pulp Magazine, YesterYearFiction, AnotheRealm Magazine, Alien Skin Magazine, on Orion's Child Science Fiction and Fantasy Magazine, Farther Stars Than These, on Digital Dragon Magazine, on Kalkion Science Fiction and Fantasy Web Magazine, on Orion's Arm, on Quantum Muse, Surprising Stories, on EMG- ZINE, on The Speculative Edge Magazine, on Australian Antipodean SF, on British Schlock!Webzine , on Australian SQ Mag, and in print inside an American Horror Anthology, title: "Now I Lay Me Down To Reap..." by Sirens Call Publications, inside a British Sci-Fi Anthology, title: "Timeless Worlds" by Schlock Magazine, inside an American Sci-Fi Anthology for short- stories, title "Yarr!- A Space Pirate Anthology" by Martinus Publishing, inside a British Sci-Fi Anthology, title: "Pulpateers" by the same publisher, inside a British Sci-Fi Anthology, title: "The Year's Best Schlock! Sci-Fi 2013" by the same publisher, inside a British Fantasy Anthology, title: "The Year's Best Schlock! Fantasy 2013" by the same publisher, inside a British Fantasy Anthology, title: "Schlock! Barbarians" by the same publisher, inside a British Horror Anthology for short- stories, title "TALES OF THE UNDEAD - Hell whore Anthology"... by Horrified Press, inside another British

Horror Anthology for short- stories, title "TALES OF THE UNDEAD- Volume II - Hell whore Anthology continues... " by the same publisher, inside a British Sci-Fi Anthology for short- stories, title "JUST ONE MORE STEP Anthology"... by the same publisher , inside another British Sci-Fi Anthology for short- stories, title "DARK IN THE LIMELIGHT"... by the same publisher, inside a British Horror Anthology for short- stories, title "PLAGUE..." by Horrified Press, inside an American Sci-Fi Anthology for shorts-stories, title: "Stories in Future Tense: The 2015 Word Branch Publishing Science Fiction Anthology", inside an American Fantasy Anthology for shorts-stories, title: "Limelight: A Golden Light Anthology" by Chambertonpublishing, inside an American Anthology of Historical/Fantasy shorts-stories by the same publisher, too, title: "Gaslight: A Golden Light Anthology", inside an American Horror Anthology for short- stories, title "Dark Light 2" by Crushing Hearts Black Butterfly Publishing, inside an American Horror Anthology for short- stories, title "Cirque d'Obscure" by the same publisher, inside an American Horror Anthology, title: "Temptations and other sins" by Fantastic Horror Press, inside an American Anthology of Urban Fantasy/Horror shorts-stories, title: "Blood and Guts: An Anthology of the Gross and Disgusting" by Static Movement Publications, inside an American Horror/Steampunk Anthology for shorts-stories, title: "Dreadful Legacies" by the same publisher, inside a Fantasy/Sci-Fi Anthology for shorts-stories, title: " LocoThology 2013: Tales of Fantasy & Science Fiction- Volume 3" by Loconeal

Publishing, inside a Horror Anthology for shorts-stories, title: " Undead Living" by Sunbury Press, and inside a new American Horror Anthology, title: "Mental Ward: Stories from the Asylum..." by Sirens Call Publications, inside an American Horror Anthology, title: "Slaughter House: The Serial Killer Edition - Volume 2", by the same publisher, inside an Australian Sci-Fi Anthology, title: "Star Quake 1 - Best of SQ Mag's 2012"- Anthology, inside a Canadian Horror Anthology, title: "Blood and Roses" by Scarlett River Press, inside an Urban Fantasy/Horror Anthology for shorts-stories, title: "Miseria's Chorale" by Forgotten Tomb Press, inside an American Anthology of Horror shorts-stories, title: "Deadhead miles" by Spook Show Publishing, inside a new British Horror Anthology, title "Night Shade- Volume I... " by Little Bird Publishing, inside another British Sci-Fi Anthology, title "Barbarians of the Red Planet" by Rogue Planet Press, inside another American Urban Fantasy/Horror Anthology, title "Sweet Dreams and Night Terrors" by Silent Fray Productions, inside another American Urban Fantasy Anthology, title "Cursed Curiosities" by Barbwire Butterfly Books, inside another Horror Anthology for short- stories, title "Undercurrents of Fear..." by the same publisher, inside another British Urban Fantasy/Horror Anthology for short- stories, title "Detectives of the Fantastic -Volume 1" by Thirteen Press, inside another British Urban Fantasy/ Horror Anthology for short- stories, title "Detectives of the Fantastic -Volume II" by the same publisher, inside another British Urban Fantasy/Horror An-

thology for short- stories, title "Detectives of the Fantastic -Volume III" by the same publisher,inside another American Horror Anthology, title "The Dead walk" by Breaking Fate Publishing, inside another British Urban Fantasy/Horror Anthology, title "Growing pains" by Sinister Saint Press, inside an American Horror Anthology for short- stories, title "Dark Light 4" by Crushing Hearts Black Butterfly Publishing, inside a British Sci-Fi/Horror Anthology for short- stories, title "LOCH SHOCK..." by Horrified Press, inside another British Horror Anthology for short- stories, title "TALES OF THE UNDEAD - Hell whore III Anthology... " , by the same publisher, inside an American Paranormal/Erotic Anthology for short- stories, title "Bloody Sexy" by Hot Ink Press, inside another British Steampunk Anthology for short- stories, title "Steamworld..." by Thirteen Press, inside another British Dark Fantasy/Horror Anthology for short- stories, title "Swords against Cthulhu..." by Rogue Planet Press, inside another British Horror Anthology for short- stories, title "How to Trick the Devil..." by Erebus Press, inside another American Horror Anthology, title: "Crossroads in the dark" by Burning Willow Press, inside an American Sci-Fi Anthology for short- stories, title "Out of Phase: Tales of Sci-Fi Horror" by Sirens Call Publications, inside an Anthology for adventurous short- stories, title "The Adventures of Pirates" by Zimbell House Publishing, inside another British Fantasy Anthology, title "Devil's Armory II" by Barbwire Butterfly Books, inside an Anthology for Urban Fantasy/Historical short- stories, title "Veil of Secrets" by the same publisher, inside another British Sci-Fi Anthology for short- stories, title "Fall of the Galactic Empire..." by Rogue Planet Press, inside a British Fantasy/Horror Anthology for short- stories, title "Swords against Cthulhu II: Hyperborean Nights" by the same publisher, inside an American Urban Fantasy/Horror Anthology for short- stories, title "ME: Haunted Love" by Macabre Maine, inside another American Sci-Fi Anthology for shorts-stories, title: "Stories in Future Tense: The 2016 Word Branch Publishing Science Fiction Anthology" , inside a Canadian Anthology of Fantasy/Horror Fairytales, title: "Incandescence Transcendent" by Oloris Media Publishing, inside an American Urban Fantasy/Horror Anthology for short- stories, title "Excite Spice Boxed Set - Science Friction" by Excite Spice- Excessica, inside another American Horror Anthology, title: "Crossroads in the dark- Volume 2- Urban Legends" by Burning Willow Press, inside a Scottish Horror/Erotic Anthology for short- stories, title "Slice Girls (Splatter Goth)" by Vamptasy Publishing, and will appear soon, in print, inside an American Sci-Fi/Steampunk Anthology for short- stories, title "Altered Europe" by Martinus Publishing, inside another British Sci-Fi/Fantasy Anthology for short- stories, title "Sword and Planet..." by Rogue Planet Press, inside another British Sci-Fi Anthology for short- stories, title "Devil's Armory III" by the same publisher, in another American Erotic Horror Anthology, title: "Have Quest, Will Travel" by Inkstained Succubus Press, inside an American

Erotic/Urban Fantasy/Horror Anthology for short-stories, title "Depraved Desires" by HellBound Books, inside an American Horror Anthology for short- stories, title "Weird Western Yarns" by Western Trail Blazer Publishing, inside an American Urban Fantasy/Horror Anthology for short- stories, title "Bite me" by Macabre Maine, inside an American Anthology for short- stories, title "Automaton: A Steampunk Anthology" by Baird Speculative Fiction, inside another American Steampunk/Horror Anthology, title: "Steampunk Monster Hunter - The Dark Monocle" by Emby Press, inside another Anthology for short- stories, title "Pets are people too..." by Fey Publishing, inside an American Anthology of Horror shorts-stories, title: "Deadhead miles- Volume 2" by Fear or Fright Publishing, inside another British Urban Fantasy/Horror Anthology for short- stories, title "Detectives of the Fantastic -Volume IV" by Thirteen Press, inside another British Urban Fantasy/ Horror Anthology, title "Music" by Sinister Saint Press, inside another British Sci-Fi/Steampunk Anthology, title "When disaster strikes" by the same publisher, inside another British Urban Fantasy/Horror Anthology, title "A door appeared" by the same publisher, inside another British Urban Fantasy/Horror Anthology, title "Strange vacations" by the same publisher, inside another British Horror Anthology, title "Teenage insanity" by the same publisher, inside another British Sci-Fi Anthology, title "Aftermath" by the same publisher, inside another British Horror Anthology for short- stories, title "Troll" by Thirteen O'

Clock Press, in another American Anthology for Fantasy short-stories, title "Hidden in Your World" by Visionary Press, inside an American Erotic/Sci-Fi Anthology for short- stories, title "Slice Girls (Reprint)" by Stitched Smile Publications, inside the American book "New Legends: Fantasy Anthology 2" by Visual Adjectives, inside the American book "New Legends: Mercenary • Engineer • Captain Book 2" by the same publisher, inside a Horror Anthology for shorts-stories, title: " Climate Fiction" by Sunbury Press, inside an American Anthology of Fantasy shorts-stories, title: "Distressing Damsels" by Fantasia divinity Magazine, in another Canadian Horror Anthology, title: "Tortured Souls Volume 1" by Scarlett River Press, inside an American Anthology of Fantasy/Horror shorts-stories of strictly lesbian and bisexual female tales, title: "Magickally Delicious" by Full Moon Books, inside an American Anthology of Horror shorts-stories, title: " Demonology" by Static Movement Publications, and then inside an American Anthology of Horror shorts-stories by the same publisher, again, title:"Love at first bite"

He is also a scale modeler who likes mostly Science Fiction and Real Space models, some of his little Dioramas have been shown also on some Italian (scale model) magazines like Soldatini, Model Time, Tutto-Soldatini and online on American site StarShipModeler, MechaModelComp, on British SFM: UK site and Italian SMF .

Some Sci-Fi/fantasy/Horror short- stories by him in Italian have been published on Alpha Aleph,

Alpha Aleph Extra, Algenib, Oltre il Futuro, Nugae 2.0, SogniHorror, La Zona Morta, edizioni Lo Scudo, Antologia Robot ITA 0.1, Antologia Il Segreto dell'Universo, Antologia E-Heroes, etc.'

Here a brief presentation of Michele DUTCHER who edited the short-story:

"Michele Dutcher, aka Bottomdweller, lives in a carriage house in Old Louisville Kentucky with her border collie – Daisy Dukes. She has a BS degree in Elementary Education from Indiana University with minors in theology & sociology and has been writing Science Fiction stories for about a decade. She edits all the first drafts of Sergio's short stories."

KEK COMES: A SONG OF UNIVERSAL CHAOS

E. W. Farnsworth

Kek, fat green one, comes with dreams of chaos.
Amphibian breeder, eclipsing moons,
Tears Intergalactic Empires' currents.
Cthulhu's hearers, long since fled despairing
Frail reason's reckoners chased through black vacuums.

Furies come behind, gnaw tangled tresses.
Shooting stars burst in powdery wakes, alas.
Here the thyrsis waves. There huge sharp shears whack.
Kek grins, slouching, many-legged, egging on
Mindless masses mingling, meandering.

Wisdom's *gravitas* abandons hybrids.

Paths for madness loom labyrinthine, glue
For those deemed free and these enthralled
alike,
While armies clash, bones and flesh sunder-
ing,
Iron edges cut, excoriating.

Souls vanish in the general melee.
Streets full of frogs and forests green turn
black.
Chartreuse fires' consumptive salamanders
Whisper in Kek's membranous tympanums
Falsehoods proclaiming green glorious rule.

Equally false myths of Cthulhu's return
To restore justice and peace join other lies.
Weak victims writhe to catch a drift and live.
Spirits rise only to fall in stellar roiling.
Kek's new worm holes suck the vast waste of
space.

Disintegration rules and ghosts swirl by:
Humans, machines, silicon and carbon,
No hope of cures for Kek's infectious plagues:
Kek croaks and groans while hope parades in
chains.
Pass by untouched armadas of the saved.

Kek cried: "I do so love the circumplex!"
Nonsense spewed from his blubbery wet lips.
"Hear truth from me. Others prevaricate."
Chirping night sounds Kek's blank suasion
holds sway.

"'Cthulhu trolls in majesty!' I, Kek, say."

Through trillions of galaxies his presence
Invades receptive minds with paradox,
His language larded with tautologies.
In his train, multitudes follow chanting,
Mindlessly mimicking. "Adore great Kek!"

"Do as I say, not as I do," Kek shouts.
"We do as you say. Lead right on!" they chant.
"Order in chaos!" is ungodly sung.
Cold and inhospitable space fills up.
Stars' supernovas seem Kek's symphony.

Through cacophony cloaked go the vessels,
Impervious yet aware of Kek's ruin.
The bloviating beast puffs out his chest.
As if he wore a quadrillion gold crowns,
Kek motions evil ends to all things good.

Nay-sayers are immediately slain.
Kek's smile consigns others to raw rending.
Confusion reigns when Kek shifts his mes-
sage.
Rage swings antipodean with Kek's words.
"Find *Arcturus* and bring its crew to me."

Hordes race in all directions seeking fame.
Kek's changing mind keeps its inconstancy.
"Forget *Arcturus*. What is it to me?"
Kek's followers fall back in line behind.
And so it goes as Kek's wild chaos brews.

Yet Kek is active, and this liked his throng.

Insane, they tore each other while they
marched.
A friend became a foe then green fodder.
Kek feasted as he spread philosophy,
Black nihilism laced with cruel rapine.

Enormous Kek grows, filling the cosmos.
His song becomes his dimensionless self.
As he views his mob, he turns and opens
wide:
His mouth absorbs detritus, scum and ash,
Washing all into his flaccid corpus.

Until Kek finds he is alone, he smiles.
His satisfaction does not last for long.
Again fawning sycophants he craves.
Into the universal void, he spews
All he has ingested, his raucous crowd.

Like tsunamis across distant waters,
Kek's rush of gabblers emerged and sang.
"Kek, you rule the universe and all time.
Take your faithful spirits with you always.
We don't worry about your bold intents."

"Follow me, faithful! Cthulhu's dead and
gone."
His rabble repeats, "Cthulhu's dead and
gone!"
The whole universe echoes, "Cthulhu's dead!"
"I, Kek, are all you know of truth. Believe!"
"We believe: Kek is all we know of truth."

Did Cthulhu and the elders hear this chant?
They did not contradict if they did hear.
Aboard *Arcturus* the Argonauts heard
Like old Odysseus tied to the mast:
Kek's folly did not tempt them from their
path.

E. W. Farnsworth is widely published on line and in print. He is a frequent contributor to Horrified Press anthologies. For further information see www.ewfarnsworth.com

KEK SQUAD

Alex S. Johnson

These days, Jambo Krumholz thought more and more about retirement.

Granted, this was a lousy idea, especially given the current economy. In fact, since he'd hung up his shingle at the World's Biggest Indoor Mall— "Got Spooks? See Jambo. Reasonable Rates, Fast Service"—he'd had more business than he knew what to do with. But things were different now than when he'd started, fresh from graduate school with a degree in Esoteric Sciences, ready to challenge the world of psychic detection with state-of-the-art techniques and his own, patented Debamboozler machine.

Then, Jambo had the field to himself. Anybody who claimed they understood how ghosts really operated, how to follow a trail of ectoplasmic slime to the victim of a genuine possession, why the right shoes were so very, very important —were forced to submit to his own superior skill set. Many pretenders had jumbled together tools that looked efficient but fell apart at the actual site of a haunting. But not now.

Jambo was only one among thousands sweeping the hallways of ancient mansions with bleeping devices, poring over tattered manuscripts, interviewing wizened witnesses of fantastic crimes. The arena of parapsychology was over-run. Everybody wanted in. And because of the glut, Krumholz looked like just another ghost dick trying to cash in on the craze.

But when he checked his bank balance, Jambo had to admit with a weary sigh that retirement wasn't in the cards. The only thing that held his professional interest now was the ongoing war between a hoary elder god—Cthulhu—and a surprise contender fresh to the block, the frog-headed deity known as Kek.

Jambo was sitting at his station in the mall, sporting an older tan suit that barely contained his bulging stomach, watching the shoppers as they poured down the walkways, when his old friend, Bone City Detective Joe Oroborus, peeked his head in the door. "Mind if I join you?" he asked.

Jambo shrugged. "Sure, why not."

Oroborus was wearing his off-duty uniform, his street clothes, which he thought made him look like a neo-gangsta, but in reality—nobody had the heart to tell him what he really looked like, an aging third-generation hippie in a Jimi Hendrix Rainbow Bridge hat, a motley scarf, ragged concert T and bell bottom jeans. He scanned Krumholz's office. "Gee, you've let yourself go," he said.

Krumholz was about to tell him to shut up, but he didn't have the strength anymore. He knew the brochures were out of date, his equipment shoddy, even his shoes ground down at the heel. Passing a hand over his round, shiny dome, he gestured to the Mr. Coffee nestled on the sink behind his desk. "Help yourself." Oroborus looked around for a clean cup, and when he didn't find one, resigned himself to the old Styrofoam. Krumholz knew BCD Oroborus didn't approve, but keeping it green was the least of his concerns.

"Say," said Krumholz finally. "Do you know anything about this Kek?"

"No more than anybody else," said Oroborus. "I mean yeah, I've seen the documentaries. He's all over the news. But what does he want? And why the frog-head?"

"Exactly." The detective's question sparked something inside him. "You know, I seem to recall a case with similar features. Remember the Haunted Museum Caper, where…"

"Yes, yes," said Oroborus. Talking shop seemed to change the parameters of their meeting. No longer was this simply a case of a pal checking in on a dispirited friend—pun subliminally intended—but a live inquiry with aspects that touched both of them professionally. Oroborus began to pace back and forth, his coffee forgotten.

"It seemed at first the Egyptology Exhibit had been burglarized, which is why neither of us were alerted. After all, a simple matter of a cracked case, a missing artifact, didn't set off any alarm bells."

"Right. But it was right after that babies started dying. Dying in droves. It was your idea to see if there was a connection between the break-in and the SIDS outbreak."

"Maybe it's time to revisit the Museum," said Krumholz.

"You read my mind," said Oroborus.

Actually, Krumholz had not read his mind on this occasion, but the literal fact of it was unimportant. What was important was the renewed sense on both sides about the cold case they'd laid to rest years before. Perhaps there were clues they'd missed the first time around that would explain who or what Kek might be, and why he had it in for Cthulhu, or the other way around.

The Haunted Museum Caper had come about as an off-shoot of the break-in, when it appeared for a while that To-Tep-Tutan, the mummy closely affiliated with Osiris, had vanished from the glass case and become invisible, the better to sneak up on visitors and try to strangle them. The mummy was recovered, a little battered but none the worse for wear; but that wasn't the salient factor connecting Kek to the crime.

On the drive over in Oroborus' unmarked

black squad car, Krumholz checked out the environs with resensitised eyes. A few raindrops began to fall, followed by a cascade, as storm-clouds gathered overhead. Lighting lit up the sky, and thunder crackled directly overhead. The gutters were filling up, and for a second, Krumholz thought he saw a mass of tiny, tailed creatures wriggling through the rain-lashed concrete channels.

He glanced up and beheld the massive billboard Omniversal Studios had erected to advertise the new movie with the old character Krommet the Frog, his style revamped to appeal to an edgier crowd. "Krommet's Back, and He's Pimpin' For Profit," ran the text.

"Jesus," Krumholz muttered.

"What happened?" asked Oroborus distractedly.

"You remember the Murpet Show, right? Back in the day… now this…" he shook an index finger in the direction of the billboard. "This travesty. Is nothing wholesome anymore?"

Oroborus laughed. "Dude, you're starting to sound like an old guy."

Krumholz folded his arms and dug his massive chin into his neck. The PD was right. He was turning into a geezer. If this kept up, maybe he should retire after all. Leave the field to the youngsters fresh out of community college with their A.A.s in Ghosting. Now it was more a trade than anything—no theory, no deeper understanding.

Then his jaw dropped.

"It's so obvious… it's been staring us in the face all along."

"What, dude, what?"

"Or maybe not." Krumholz's face fell. A look of dawning horror crawled across his features.

"Um… are you okay, man?"

Krumholz shifted in his seat, smacked himself on the cheeks. "Yeah, yeah. Dude, I'll be fine. I just had this intimation of cosmic dread. But I'm good."

"Shit," said Oroborus.

"What? Did you see him?"

"The parking lot is full. Wait… wha? See who?"

"Never mind that right now," said Krumholz.

He looked up. His friend was right. They'd have to park at the multilevel garage next to the museum, which charged an arm and a leg—a minimum ten bucks for an hour. The museum lot was full of vehicles with stickers and stencils that established the driver as a member of the Ghosting fraternity. You couldn't go anywhere now without running into them.

My God, thought Krumholz. Who you gonna call? Pick a number.

The only free space in the parking garage was located right under the roof, and by the time they'd limped out the back door to the walkway that ran between the garage and the museum, they were dripping enough sweat to contend with the rain. Again, Krumholz noted the mass of wigglers in the gutter along the boulevard that ran parallel to the museum complex.

"Tadpoles, man. Freaking tadpoles."

Oroborus shrugged. "So what's your point?"

"Isn't that a little bit... I don't know, unusual?"

"Well, one or two is normal. What are you driving at?"

"Never mind." Oroborus didn't get it either. Krumholz fumbled with the clasp on his umbrella and finally pushed it open. The PD just hunched over and scooted along, raindrops splashing on long blonde locks. When they got to the museum foyer, Krumholz looked for the Director's Office.

"Shit, everything's changed around."

"Maybe we should have Googled, or called ahead, or something," offered Oroborus.

Krumholz found the gold plaque in the green faux-marble tiling next to the elevators. The Director's office had indeed moved, but not far. They rode to the third floor in silence, like two surly teenagers who'd just had a fight. The tension between them was odd, because they'd always gotten along so well before.

But Oroborus seemed like he was on a different planet. Or another solar system.

"Ah yes, I see," said the Director absently, when the pair strode in the door without knocking. "Your manners haven't improved. Besides that, how may I assist you?" The Director looked even more ancient, even crumbling, than he had three years' previous.

"I, we…" sputtered Krumholz haltingly.

"But please, take a seat. Do you like what I've done with the place?"

Krumholz cringed at the Director's lavender tie and the thick clouds of perfume that poured off his pink suit. He hoped it wasn't homophobia or anything nasty like that that instilled his dislike of the man. He thought it was perhaps his artificiality, as though he were frozen in an Edwardian drawing room scene.

Oroborus, still standing, came to the point. "My colleague and I think you may be able to help us with this Kek matter."

"Why yes, certainly." The Director rubbed his hands together. Krumholz detected a shine of fresh hand cream on the man's long fingers. "In fact, I had a feeling you might be coming over. Please pardon the shuttered windows, but I've been suffering from hypersensitivity to the light. And at my age…"

How old was he, really? Krumholz remembered from their previous encounter he'd almost suspected the Director himself of being the mummy, but then banished the thought as crazy. Now, he wasn't so sure. There was darkness at the core of the man's being, a darkness that spoke of horrors and writhing tentacles, of stellar wars and shattered spaceships. Debris floating in the haunted insect void. He wondered if Oroborus could see what he saw. Possibly, but if so, he sure as hell wasn't letting on.

He realized with a shock that there was a distinct disconnect between the Director's lip movements and his voice, which sounded as though it were coming from some place *beyond the room*.

"The missing artifact," said Oroborus flatly. "It was a figurine of Heqet, wasn't it?"

"Indeed," said the Director.

Krumholz was suddenly engulfed with panic. His heart hammered in his chest. On the drive over, and even on the way in, Oroborus appeared oblivious to all the signs—the tadpoles in the gutter, the billboard with Krommet, the appearance, over and over again, of a vast universal conspiracy that told them Kek was Heqet, the Egyptian fertility goddess, and that she, not Cthulhu, now ruled Earth and all its creation.

"Ankh sign to Hatshepsut in one," said Oroborus obliquely, as though he were describing some obscure Egyptian chess rite.

The Director chuckled. "Oh yes, She is the goddess of us all. She reigns supreme. Those who pray to her and consecrate sacrifice in her name gain powers the likes of which little people like you could never dream." He directed this last bit directly to Krumholz.

Then Krumholz knew that every moment of his life for the last three years had led to this precise moment, when he was led to understand that no new life would come again without the stamp of Heqet, She who was Kek before and was again; the frog-headed goddess of the Egyptians who ushered babies forth here and in the next world.

The light in the office dimmed, and the Director's pink jacket glowed. Puckers in his face burst, and from them poured a cascade of tadpoles that slithered across the desk. Meanwhile, Oroborus' jaw had gained a distinctly amphibious caste.

"You wondered what your role in life was, now that occult investigation is the flavour of the week. Whether you should retire. Am I wrong?"

"I—no, you're not wrong," said Krumholz. Oroborus smiled, his eyes bulging. "But I don't understand… what's happening to me?"

"The fate of all who meddle in the domain of Kek," said the Director. "Your search for the culprit, the babykiller, was too successful. Now, for the protection of all who bear her mark, you must be returned to her. Don't think of it as death. Think of it as another chance. One quick hop to another lily pad, as it were."

"Merciful heavens protect us," whispered Krumholz, who watched as a thick gelid slime began to crawl over his skin, encasing him in a translucent web. Stars like jewel points shone in the sudden void, and he was floating through space in a jelly coffin, a tail having spouted from his coccyx.

He would have his retirement, all right, after traveling through the twelve gates of the afterlife, accompanied by a man in a motley scarf and another in a pink suit and a face made of tadpoles, who smelled of cloying perfume and artifice.

Osiris, ithyphallic and bearded, in mummied form, lieth upon his bier; over his feet and his body hover two hawks. At the head kneels Hathor, who weepeth for her brother, and at the foot is a frog, symbol of the goddess Heqet.

— Willis Budgey, E.A. 1904, *Gods of the Egyptians: Volume 2*, p. 136

Alex S. Johnson is a former English college instructor. He currently runs Riot Dogg Editing Services and Nocturnicorn Books, an indie press specializing in speculative literature. His published works include the books The Doom Hippies, Brides of Doom, Bizarrely Departed *and* Skull Vinyl. *Johnson resides in Sacramento, California, USA.*

MISGIVINGS OF A BLIND MIND'S EYE

Nathan J.D.L. Rowark

Ah, that euphoric feeling of relief, the moment my hands fall to my sides, baton dropped to those left in motion.

Tap out, to tap in the next unfortunate soul stranded among the ever busy working class.

1% survey from the security of their delusional, bubble-glassed control rooms—every day at the top leaves so much further for them to fall.

A victimless crime leaves ALL victims of the greater machine, its mechanics of passive-aggressive appeasement and abandonment.

The television has begun to sound like aggravated bees, swarm contained in the back of my antiquated set piece.

Internet became an advertiser's paradise littered with cat-litter ads. Felines play while their human masters stoop to their wishes on a loop.

By glare of the image that beams from the dark
I foresee something else through armchair slumber.
My legs twitch furiously as I dream of catching a
mouse—the mouse being me.
I've been on that wheel too long, spokes worn and
paint flecks penetrating toenails black and blue.
The pressure has built again, swollen joints and no
cheese for my worries.
I wake in a sweat, but who's to care?
Cthulhu promised me oblivion, but he seems to
have forgotten me. Kek delivered me chaos—no
guarantees to where the dice would fall.
I thought one would cancel the other, would stop
this delusion and give me clarity of sight again.
But the old Gods are not forgiving of our interfer-
ence in the natural order, found unwilling to even
out an age-old equation.
After-all, it was our vote that killed us!
Should have known better than to call on either of
them, but when in a cage forged by dark forces...
I needed something bigger to allay our enemies—
we all did!
We took the red pill too willing, ignoring the dangers documented by Egyptian scholars and Pagan
heretics.
Now we shall ALL be committed to the never-end-
ing sea.
I think I can see Cthulhu at my open door now, or is
it my sanity's perception?
He's standing under the arch, bathed in half-light.

Slime drips from his tentacled limbs, along my newly laid wooden floor slats.

His working day is over—it seems. He's late!

I haven't even put the dinner on—polymer trays of burnt offerings.

Kek is with him, arm around his shoulder.

After gazing upon my dishevelled form, he throws back and lets out a hearty shriek.

Am I the last now?

"Who's going to open up the Earth tomorrow, for I don't have keys? Not within my pay grade."

Now he's smiling... HE'S BLOODY SMILING!

The lols are taking me over, and I must admit... I do feel pretty good... great again... even!

Or uneven... desperate... lonely... afraid... more out of control than ever... bathed in absurdity, cleansed by my own mediocrity!

REEEEEEEEEEEEEEEEEEEEEEEEEEEEEEEEEEE-EEEEEE!

Nathan J. D. L. Rowark lives in London. He writes horror stories and hopes to become a literary terror writer.

THE WIND IN MY FIST, THE WAVES OF MY MOUTH

by Helen E Davis

We could not talk under the waves, only sing, and the Others couldn't stand the salt. So we met at the boundary, where the land crumbled into the sea, where the air tasted of sand and seaweed, not quite one realm or the other. There, at tables splintered by broiling summers and frozen winters, in the lee of a weathered shack that had served beer and spirits to us for generations, we aired our concerns to each other and drank to the future. The nights passed quietly on that sliver of sand bound by stone cliffs, on an ocean-locked rock barely within sight of the mainland, for the primitive people knew not to come.

They had learned to avoid the unseasonal storms that raked the black rocks, the hot, dry winds that stirred devils from the sand, the sudden tides that surged over the tide-word pebbles to the wind-swept grasses, then retreated, leaving strange twisted forms and globs of iridescent, putrid flesh. They knew to avoid the bright red jellyfish, whose stingers left circular contusions that blackened and decayed within their living flesh, and the small, prickly barbs that sent fevers and chills into their blood. But mostly, they knew to avoid *us*.

Until that night, in the midst of the blackfish runs, when it was business rather than pleasure that drew us out of the undulating waves before the moon had risen.

"Reunion, shemuion," Midwest Dave muttered. He yanked down his Gore-Tex hat to cover his eyes. "It was completely, utterly lousy."

"Do tell us," Rocky Point Dave sighed. He picked at the rip on the sleeve of his own ancient rubber coat where the original owner—who had no more need of it, or anything, ever again—had been caught by the broken beam of a shattered ship. "We never, ever tire of the details."

"*He* hasn't heard it." Midwest Dave pointed at Sheena, who wore a heavily stained canvas coat. So much for the idea that cold salt water gets out blood. "Right, Boston Dave?"

"I'm a *she*," Sheena insisted. The youngest among us, she often forgot that her body was now shaped like a barrel, and that the flatness of her face hid her other features.

"Okay," Midwest Dave muttered, as much of an apology as he ever gave. "*She* hasn't heard it."

I glanced out at the darkness, hoping to see the Others, but could see only rocks and the grass whipping in the sea wind. Surf rolled in the darkness, bringing waves of salt and rotted seaweed-infused air to wash over us. My skin itched, drying out and irritated by my wool coat, once red but now faded to rose. I absently scratched my arm with my other webbed hand.

"The place was ruined, totally ruined." Midwest Dave leaned his head back to pour his pale piss beer into his wide mouth. He pounded the empty enamel mug on the table to signal that it was empty. "Drainage installed in Wilder Bowl—no more swamp! Instead, flowers everywhere! And these disgusting trees with huge leaves."

Rocky Point Dave rolled his huge eyes at us. He missed the forest, he had told me once. Kelp and sea weed just wasn't the same.

"And the dining halls—all these little artisanal cafes instead of one big, friendly Scum. Preppies everywhere. At least the weather was normal, rain and mist every day."

Sheena tipped her Mimosa into her mouth, spilling a bit. She was only just learning how to drink without lips. "What's a Preppie?"

Such a child. "What you would call a fashionista. They were very ambitious and dressed, well, like that."

The Others had arrived, and with them the wind turned dry, blowing down from the rocks to challenge the sea, stinking of myrrh and old money. The Kek wore black linen suits, cut narrow, and black ghutras secured with white igals. Gold bracelets, set with chronometers, glittered on their wrists, shimmering smoothness against their twisted, lumpy skin that looked as if a dread disease had ravaged their bodies. Five steps behind and two steps to the left of each one, the Kauket glided over the sand. Each wore a shimmering sheath dress overlaid by a lacy shawl, and translucent scarves, fluttering at their edges, wrapped across their faces like veils. Thumb-sized gems, their brilliance matching their owners eyes, hung from heavy gold necklaces.

Rocky Point Dave gaped at the sight, his huge eyes almost falling out of his flat face.

"Shut your mouth," I warned him. "You look like a fish."

He shot a sour look at me, but he did shut his mouth. Then he muttered, "Last time I saw them, the girls were all in those head-to-toe gowns. Now they look—wow!"

"Burqa," Sheena muttered back. "And you have fry at home."

"Can't blame a man for using his eyes."

To tell the truth, I don't mind that we don't talk beneath the waves.

Chike, the older and squatter of the Kek, approached me and bowed. "A fortuitous evening, Boston Dave. May the Great Gods look upon us with favour."

I touched my wool stocking cap. "May the gods ignore us. Sit down."

He took the place opposite me. Ini-herit—younger, taller, with shoulders as wide as a topsail, sat down next to Chike. He was the quiet one, but the one you did not insult. The two Kauket settled at the other end of the table, closer to Sheena than the rest of us. Only the colour of their slit-pupil eyes distinguished them, emerald green for Sekhet and topaz blue for Gamila.

Chike pressed his fingers, fat at the tips, together. "And who is your new companion?"

"I'm Sheena," she stated.

His eyes bulged, and then he shifted his gaze back to me. "That is a female's name, is it not?"

"Keep her quiet, Rocky Point," I muttered, loud enough for Sheena to hear. "They don't like noisy women."

She snorted back, and I had one of my rare longings for the ability, long lost, to smile.

The Barman, an almost skeletal shape inside baggy clothes, his face buried beneath bushy beard and eyebrows, his head hidden by a tangled mat of white hair, hustled out with a tray of fresh drinks. A fresh Mimosa for Sheena, lager for Midwest Dave, whisky for Rocky Point Dave, and for me, grog. The Kek and Kauket took wine, blood-red and heady, poured from a large decanter into tiny crystal cups. And then the Barman set down a large plate of food—dates, fried bread balls, pickled fish, and seaweed-wrapped bundles, along with small dishes of red, black, and green sauce.

"What is *this?*" Rocky Point Dave asked. He poked one of the bundles.

"Something new," the Barman mumbled in a voice like a gate, unoiled, swinging on a rusty post.

"New?" We all turned to stare at him, our eyes bulging in dismay. The Kauket shuddered, waves rolling up and down their sinuous bodies, and the Kek croaked. Except for Sheena, who scooped up half of the rolls in one wide hand and tossed them all into her mouth.

We turned to look at her.

"California Rolls," she squealed. "It's been *ages.*"

"Very popular," the Barman intoned.

Not with our kind, I didn't think, unless the young ones had taken to sneaking up on the beach at night, after the moonset. Perhaps that was why the Kek had called the meeting? I waved the bar-keeper away, then looked into Chike's slit-pupil eyes. "You asked to talk?"

"It's a good night, very pleasant." He placed a pickled fish onto his tongue, then swallowed. His eyes bulged as the morsel went down. "Is that not reason enough to meet with good company and pass the darkness?"

To this the Kauket giggled, their laughter like air escaping from rubber balls.

"My skin is drying out, and my companions are not." I shrugged toward Midwest Dave, who was already staring at the bottom of his mug. "The moon will be up before long, and we haven't the time to play games."

"Very well," Chike sighed. "If you must be rude about it. We ask for the beach this month."

Sheena's hand stopped mid-way to the rest of the rolls. "No way! We were planning a big fall party to usher in the season!"

I waved her down. Only the young are anxious to do this month what can easily be done next month. "So you wish to trade?"

"No. We wish to take it in payment."

Sudden raucous laughter erupted from behind me. I turned, along with the others, to see that our sanctum had been invaded. Two primitive males and a three primitive females, the latter wearing less clothes than even our youngest fry, lounged at one of the three remaining tables. They noticed us, and one of the males called out, "Wattaya looking at, fish-eyes?"

More raucous laughter.

It was time, perhaps, for a fresh scourging of the sands. After our business was concluded, of course, for the salt water would sting the others as badly as the primitives. I turned my back on the apes and pushed my mug from one webbed hand to the other. "By what right do you claim we owe you our beach?"

"For your trespasses upon our property." Chike's gaze stayed steady on my face. "For the damage wreaked by your people upon our yachts."

In the corner of my eye, I saw that Sheena was suddenly preoccupied with the tray of food. As she pulled it close and began to closely examine the rice and seaweed rolls, I understood what had happened. Young people and their pranks. Why else would any of us have entered those creaking, mouldy wrecks stinking of green water and stale fish? "The boats that were sailing in *our* waters?"

"On your waters. You own only what is beneath the surface."

Midwest Dave put one of the pickled fish in his mouth, and shuddered. He grabbed up his mug, peered inside, and banged it loudly on the table. I looked for the Barman, but saw that he was busy handing out beer cans to yet another group of primitives, giving them the attention that was due to us. "Your keels rest *in* the water, and are therefore part of our domain."

"You must leave your domain, as you define it, to enter ours. By your logic, all land beneath sea level is your domain."

Yes, the French Quarter of New Orleans definitely belonged to us, and had for decades. Unfortunately, the primitives had learned how to keep the day going all through the night, with their music and their bright lights thrown out into the street. But we still claimed the shadowed spots, as well as anything that wandered into them. "We do."

Ini-herit took a handful of the pickled fish and ate them all at once, his gaze on Midwest Dave all the while. He did not reach for his drink afterwards. Midwest Dave reached out, took an equal number, dredged them through the pungent green sauce, and swallowed them together. His eyes bulged out, and stayed bulged out, but he did not reach for his mug. It was still empty, anyway.

"It is more than that your people are entering our ships. They are consuming our food, our wine, and frightening the Kaukek."

Sekhet watched me with her emerald eyes, her gaze steadfast even as she lifted her glass behind her scarf to drink. Gamila had turned to Sheena, and was accepting a pair of dates from her. Long fingers, faintly scaled, brushed webbed, skeletal hands, paused briefly, drew smoothly away.

"Terrifying them," Ini-herit added.

The Barman arrived with fresh drinks and another plate of food, which he almost threw down on the table. He gave Midwest Dave a full pitcher of lager.

Rocky Point Dave leaned closer. "If you drank the real stuff, you wouldn't need so much."

"It *is* real!" Midwest Dave croaked back. "None of that three-point-two piss here!"

Lager always looked like piss to me. Tasted

like it, too. I turned my attention back to Chike. "Your boats are scaring our squids. Driving off our fish. Distressing our sharks. They do not belong in our waters, and if they come, we have every right to take payment from them."

"Hey, keep!" a primitive yelled, one of a group that had claimed the last table. The numbers had swelled at the other tables as well, and they were growing in noise as well as boorish behaviour. The first group had started throwing white balls into red cups, and the second was playing a game with dice and shots of whiskey.

"Keep!" the primitive screamed again. "Turn on the damn box!"

And then, as if these monkey were the masters of the waves and wind, not just the stunted remnants of a failed experiment, the Barman hobbled over to his window, picked up a wand, and waved it at a frame that was suddenly full of noise and colour.

Rocky Point Dave looked up from his drink. "Would you look at that?"

"It's just a TV." Midwest Dave tried one of the fried balls. He took another. "Haven't you seen a TV?"

"Not with colour," Rocky Point Dave replied.

"It's the Weather Channel," Sheena sighed. "Oh, look, a hurricane is headed for Florida. Big surprise."

The Kaukek turned in unison, smoothly to see the box. Ini-herit followed their gaze, but

Chike stared at me. His fingers were pressed so hard together that the ends were white. "Our small boats, on the surface of the water, cannot be scaring the fish down where you live."

"They may be small, but they make a lot of noise." My last words were drowned by a roar of voices.

"What?" Chike asked.

"A lot of noise!" I shouted back, my words now echoing in a sudden silence.

"Who's making a lot of noise, you big freak!" screamed a primitive. He swaggered out of his seat, more paunch than punch, and stood with his fat arms akimbo. "You gonna shut me up?"

Giggles and shrieks followed his threat.

I turned to face him, showing the full of my altered face. The primitives stared back, wide-eyed and slack-jawed, faces paling to the colour of the sand. In the silence, there was only the artless chatter of the box and the roar of the surf, each preparing to do battle with the other.

They should have run.

Instead, they pulled out their hand-boxes and held them up, as if they could ward away what about to befall them.

"Those meagre talismans will not protect you from our wrath," I roared, and took a step forward.

Behind me, Sheena coughed. "Uh, those are phones. They're filming us."

"Give us a good one, swamp-monster!"

"Hey, fishie, fishie! Wanna dance?"

"God! You look so real!" The last was a squeal from a piece of underage sharkbait.

"Perhaps we should meet again another time," Chike announced.

His party were on their feet, ready to walk up the beach and back into their territory—but they did not move fast enough. A rough swept in from the side and snatched away Sekhet's veil, then waved it over his head. "I got it! I got it!"

The Kauket covered her face with her hands, but not before we all saw the flat curve of her face, with slits where a primitive's nose would be, and the forked tongue darting out between her lip-less jaws. She had no hair, just the smooth scales of her kind, black where tresses should have fallen on her neck and shoulders, pale in the oval of her face.

"Snake-lady!" the rough called out—and laughed.

At least the Barman had the sense to run inside his shack and close the door.

Gamila raised her hands, clenched her fists. Lightening tore through the sky, and hit far too close for my comfort. I felt the thunder roll through my bones. Sharkbait and two others screamed, but the rest laughed and kept their handboxes high.

"We scour the beach!" I sang to my companions, and put forth the song that called the waters up onto the land. The other Daves joined in, and we keened in tones too high for the primitives to hear—but they could smell the dark water as it surged up, and they could feel the pounding of the waves on the rocks. The Kek and Gamila drew talismans from the pockets and intoned ancient words over them, calling forth the wind that tore down the beach, flinging aside all that was in its way. When the water met the wind, they both stopped, piling up against each other.

Beneath that rising wall of black water and white foam, its surface cut by an occasional grey fin, the primitives huddled with each other, crabs before the onrushing tide. The Kek swelled with power, their wind gusting against us, and silver fish showered out to flip in puddles of beer. We raised our voices and the dark shadow of a whale passed behind the wall.

The primitives waved their hand boxes, as if those talismans could protect them.

As the Kek clutched at the air, a hand of octopuses dropped to the beach, their arms rippling toward the screeching primitives. We pitched our voices higher, dragging the surge up and pulling the cephalopods back into the brine. Salt spray rained down on us, moistening us, strengthening us, though the Kek darted back as if stung.

"Stop!" Sheena screamed, as the Kauket with her cried out in sibilant tones.

We called for eels, which the Kek pushed out upon the sand, and the red jellyfish as large as a man's head, which the gusts pushed back into the water.

"Stop, damnit!" Sheena screeched again. She held her hat onto Gamila's head with both of her large hands. "Stop!"

I left the Daves to hold the tide and fixed her with my gaze. "In the name of Dagon, stop your nonsense and join in!"

"No!" she screamed back, showing her age in her defiance. "In the name of Dagon *and* Sekhmet, work together!"

The Kauket also shouted in her language, and I could feel the wind slack. The waters rushed in to fill the void, then also slid back into the empty ocean.

"You shitting me?" screamed the rough who waved Gamila's scarf like a signal flag. He turned to his companions. "You getting any of this?"

"This is so going on my feed!" shouted a girl who held her handbox high and pirouetted beneath it.

"Work together!" Sheena shouted again. "Wind and water in the same direction!"

But the wind dried us out and the Kek could not stand the salt. And yet—I remembered what Sheena had said. A hurricane, a beast of wind and water, a force that could not be stopped but could be called. It was far and it was strong, but there were eight of us, Dagonites and Kek together. I caught Chike's eye, then looked at the box of swirling colours.

Chike nodded. "The wind in my fist."

"The waves of my mouth."

Together we reached to the beast, and bolstered with the power of our deities, and all the souls we had claimed along the way, all the drowned sailors and mummified soldiers, swimmers caught in riptides and travellers suffocated in windstorms, all together we caught the storm and turned it toward our tiny spit of sand.

And then, even as the primitives hooted and laughed, we bade goodbye and returned to our haunts, knowing that the sea storm, as sea storms do, would creep upon them unawares and drown them with no place to run to.

Blackfish season passed on, and we were into shrimp season when the summons came again from the Kek—as I had expected it to come every day after seeing Gamila's topaz necklace around Sheena's neck. By the dark of the month we dragged up from the surf, salt water dripping from our hats and coats. The Others came to meet us, and Sheena waved warmly to Gamila.

"There they are!" screamed a primitive.

"Make the sea do that thing again!" shouted another, a barely dressed female.

Midwest Dave turned his head from side to side. "Don't think I'll be getting a drink tonight. Shack's gone."

It had been replaced by something with chrome and glass, and loud music spilled out through open windows. Other huts and structures stood or were being built where there had been only rocks and grass, and a long wooden pier stretched out into the water. Boats crowded the wood as thickly as primitives covered the sand, and where there had once been jellyfish and crabs, there now were discarded paper cups.

"Why didn't the hurricane wash them all away?" I snarled.

"They evacuated," Sheena said, as if it were something I should know.

"But—how did they know to leave before the storm?"

"Satellites, duh." She pointed to where a man was standing at the centre of a collection of boxes and wires. "Look—it's that cute guy from the weather channel!"

"I wanna see the fishies!" howled a small child, tugging at his mother's hand. "I wanna play with the fish people!"

Rocky Point Dave gave him his hungriest smile. "Do you think there is mustard and ketchup in that place?"

"See, he's friendly! He wants to play with me."

Chike stood in front of me. "We need to talk. Somewhere."

A long, lanky primitive spoke to his companion. "The weirdest weather on earth, I promise. In the Guinness book of records, even."

"Coooool," his somewhat shorter, heavily bearded companion replied. "When does the show start?"

"Not here," I told the Kek. "It's gone."

"We cannot follow you beneath the waves. We cannot stand the salt."

"We cannot live within the dry of your sands."

Beside us, Sheena and Gamila were embracing in a very friendly way, and all the primitives were waving handboxes at them. Someone waved a rainbow flag, and the two waved back.

"We have ships," Chike said.

"They are in our waters," I replied.

"Yes," he croaked. "A realm we both claim."

"Our new boundary."

"Is there beer?" Midwest Dave cried out. "Unless there's beer..."

"Tomorrow night," Chike said firmly. He glanced again at the Kek and the Dagonite, still embracing. "And if there is not what you wish, let it be on the young, our young—for they seem to have already set things to their own satisfaction."

As so, sea foam swirling around our flat finned feet, we left the world of men.

We could not meet beneath the sea, for the Others could not take the salt, and we could not meet in the desert, for we could not take the dry. And so we met on the ships, held within a circle of wind of water that kept the primitives away, surrounded by carnivorous jellyfish and venomous lizards, and there we toasted the future, fin and scale raised as one.

Helen E Davis was born in Louisiana, and earned her BA at Oberlin College, where she swears she met at least one descendant of Innsmouth inhabitants. She currently lives in Dayton Ohio with her knitting, her cats, and her husband. Her most recent book, <u>Maroon Sunia: Barbarian Princess of the Frozen North</u>, is available as an ebook in the Kindle Store and will soon be published in paperback.

TITANOMACHY

Alfred D. Byrd

Mortal, we live surrounded by doom
From realms that lie beyond our vision.
Ancient Egypt dimly descried them;
Deities only partly like us
Knew words and signs that took them be-
tween
This world of ours and locales beyond
Our skill to name or even conceive.
Beyond our homeland, conflicts arise
That shake our world and leave us perplexed:
Little know we of space and of time,
And those are only the start of things.

When we think of wars beyond our ken,
We dream of heroes, helpers, saviours—
Paladins taking our part for love
Will raise their light to counter darkness.
Maybe, when told of Kek's arising,
Meeting Cthulhu, whose death has died,
We hope for the god of frogs to keep
Our world, beloved, yet frail, intact.
We fail to grasp the nature of Kek:

Primeval darkness being his home,
What use has he for the likes of us,
Conceited creatures changing the earth
To suit our fancies—to make a mess?

He is, however, closer to us
Than the one with whom he comes to fight.
Iä, fhtagn! The Dreamer awakes
To claim dominion taken from him
By stars assuming lethal patterns
Drowning R'lyeh for aeons untold.
The stars are right for R'lyeh to rise,
And, now, immortals will cast the dice
For stakes comprising ages and worlds.
The god of frogs defies Cthulhu.
Continents shudder, tempests arise,
And the seas erase their bounds in rage.

Until the conflict subsides, we'll wait
To learn who'll strip from us our empire.
Titans contending, humans must hide
And hope for the best, but fear the worst
Because, we've learned, whatever happens,
Mortal, we live surrounded by doom.

Alfred D. Byrd has a bachelor's degree in Medical Technology from Michigan State University and a master's degree in Microbiology from the University of Kentucky. He have worked for the past more than thirty years as a research analyst in a plant genetics laboratory at the University of Kentucky.

His first published short story, "The Earth-Shaker's Answer," appeared in Quest for Atlantis. His first accepted short story, "Natural Law," appeared in Warrior Wisewoman 3. He has published as e books works of fantasy, science fiction, theology, and Appalachian regional fiction available from Amazon and other on-line booksellers. He has also published his Mythos short fiction, set largely in Kentucky, in Blue Moon of Cthulhu, available at https://www.amazon.com/Blue-Moon-Cthulhu-Alfred-Byrd-ebook/dp/B07B7XYSSB

THE WOMB

Mark Slade

I saw them going in and coming out of the naked, soft green landscape, a tunnel of light positioned in between her thighs. She laid on her back, admiring the blue-green sky. Her pert breasts were more than a handful, and her erect nipples as sharp as razor blades. Her hair was a long flowing river of ever changing colours. To youthful male eyes, she was a redhead. Men middle aged, she was most likely a strawberry blonde. In elder state, she was a cold, dark haired mistress, who teased with her charms and lured them with beautiful, haunting song—often giving them a cold hand death.

To me, she was yellow leathery fleshy monster with red bulging eyes and free-flowing tentacles, with the head of a Toad. Depending on where the sun had shifted, *SHE* would morph into a *HE*, and rear its head, mouth wide open to receive its followers souls, enabling the creature meld with the Earth, powers it received when the nuclear bomb was detonated.

Kek, is what it is called. The God/Goddess of Chaos that had led a faction of the Egyptian people to their ruin in the olden days. The androgynous God/Goddess had come back to take what was theirs when the world came to an end.

I watched the people entering and exiting her tunnel. She parted her lips and accepted the kiss from the hot sun with a deep sigh, and bathed in the gentle winds that caressed her supple body. Happy, sad, demented. All walks of life, all colours, and from all religious provocations. All of them lost in the indignation that one day, they too will fall by the wayside of memory.

I watch from a top of the hill and tremble in fear that I should not approach her, or the people for that matter. In the distance, beyond the hill I stood upon, I could hear the harpies sing. They are her protectors. They are her worshippers as well, and they are the ones who collect us, the ones who seek her out to accept the present of whatever is promised by that horrible salesman Kyled Khael. He promises wealth, lost love, lust, greed, and of course murder of that rival or loved one that turned betrayer. He brought us to the edge of the black seaside, never going further than the bridge. The Harpies flew off. Something frightened them away. Kyled tried to bring them back, screaming at them and waving his hands. We locked eyes and he knew why they had flown off.

I was promised the love of a new lover whom I could not steal.

Kyled Khael took her from me too. He promised her dead family would be returned to her. She saw the beauty of that creature, became mystified. Deranged. Soon, she became something other than human.

She became one of those in-humans. She'd been a neighbour of mine. A young girl of twenty, whom I thought needed protecting. She cared for her dead family. Made them food, even though they could not eat anymore. She changed their clothes, even though their ravaged bodies didn't need to wear them anymore. She kept their bodies' fresh with as much ice as she could find. Eventually, ice became scarce, along with other supplies. I thought she couldn't understand that they were all dead, brothers, sister, mother, father, grandmother. The truth was, she didn't want to understand. She lived in a house of denial, but deep down knew they were all dead. That was how Kyled was able to snare her.

He almost got me, too. If it were not for my new friends, members of the Legion of Cthulhu. Rat and Miriam were high ranking members. And they helped me out of Kyled's trance. We worked together to disenfranchise the followers on the west coast, destroy that part of Kek's hold over the Pacific ocean and those lands that had not been swallowed by the ocean. We'd become very close, the three of us. Miriam fancied me. But I could never make love to a chemically enhanced woman that still had the appearance of a man. I fancied Rat. But she was too involved in the cause to commit after one night of lovemaking in front of the fire we made earlier while camped in a landfill.

The world came to an end last year. Everyone scrambled to make sense of their new life. Most of us tried to carry on as if nothing had changed. As if nuclear warheads had not devastated most of the world, and walking past grey skinned, bony people eating the dead on our way to a job that no longer existed. The fact that our children no longer had legs or the polluted air had rotted out their lungs. We kissed our wives, husbands, girlfriends, boyfriends, loved ones... who were missing the left side of their mouths, and only a slimy, green tongue that remained outside their faces. We drove cars with missing doors, or the back half burned out; and cars that only ran on fumes because gasoline had been confiscated by a self-titled militia.

When the bombs fell, they awoke a monster that claimed this world as its own, and yet became the world, consumed the land, became one with the land, making the land its flesh.

I noticed something about the people that came out of the womb. Their faces had changed. Their eyes were red bulging soft balls. Their skin had become leathery yellow, and had large sores scattered across their foreheads and necks, emitting a greenish pus. Two tentacles had replaced their noses, and would move about on its own.

The people that came from the monsters womb would approach others that hadn't made it that far. These new monsters would attack the people being corralled, hold them down while those hideous tentacles would sprout five sharp prongs and drill into their foreheads. I had to cover my ears so I wouldn't hear the screams of the innocent. Still, I couldn't tear my eyes from viewing those horrible deaths. After drilling into the peoples skulls, the tentacles would pull brain matter through those silver dollar sized holes and store it in their cheeks.

Kyled Khael slithered up to me, dragging his broken legs like a snake drags his lower body across the desert sand. He was dressed in all black. Black trench coat, black vest and black shirt with black dress pants and black cowboy boots. He carried in his hands a black attaché case, where he held pamphlets of every human desire, where the photographs move to hypnotize the victims of his perpetual con game. He had two eight balls in an otherwise sunken, desolate, white, eye sockets. He had a small thin mouth sewn with black ragged string in a zig zag mouth, so only a mechanical voice came from a tiny speaker above his Adams apple.

"You should join them," he hissed, his eight ball eyes danced in the clear white sockets, then settled on two smiley faced pupils. "Sitting out of the fun can only damage the human spirit."

"What do you know of human spirit?" I said. Kyled's eight ball eyes jumped and danced again, this time settling on the skull and bones poison warning for pupils. "I see what is happening. You and that monster are enslaving people."

"They," he hissed, as a smile transformed into a frighteningly dark frown on a powder white face. "They agreed to this, as you did, for a price."

"And did you, Mr. Khael, pay them as you promised?" I said, cocking my head to the side, waiting for the right answer to my question.

"Everything they ever wanted is paid in full," Kyled hissed, bringing a black gloved, crooked finger to his forehead. "It's all up here, my friend. All dreams, hopes and human desires, perhaps in-human desires… all of it given to them as they are transformed into my masters image… they see themselves as masters of their own reality." When Kyled laughed it sounded like a V-8 engine cough-ing up crud, fumes, oil and other smog embed-ded deep in the engine. "You would have had your prize if you had not joined those terrorists."

"Hmm. Funny. We don't see ourselves as ter-rorists, Mr. Khael," I told him, pulling up my shirt and revealing my latest weapon attached to my already exposed heart and lungs. The creature gurgled, breathing irregular. It sighed, nervously jumped up and down, draining fluid from me. Horribly, discoloured pink flesh. It was wrapped around my organs like an octopus' tentacles.

Kyled step back from me, nearly tripping over his own feet. He held his hands up as if to protect himself. "Get away from me with that thing! You people are crazy!"

"Yeah," I laughed. "This shithouse is going up in flames, and Earth will go back to normal."

At that point, my new comrades in arms pulled up in their tank. Rat and Miriam. The trap door popped open and Miriam emerged, her .22 Luger fired once, a single bullet caught Kyle between the eyes. Green liquid squirted from the silver-dollar sized hole. He groaned, flesh melted from a steel, robotic frame. He wobbled, then fell to the ground.

Rat aimed the tank at the free roaming in-humans exiting the creature's womb. The tank mowed them down in streams of tens. Arms and legs were severed, flew in the air above Miriam's head. He climbed out of the trap door, his ballroom gown flowing behind him. With his right hand, Miriam held onto the rungs of the ladder that was welded to the side of the World War II M3 Stuart, and fired the Luger just as the tank's gun sprayed. One by one, the in-humans were riddled with bullets, all of them fell into huge piles on the ground.

The in-humans were slaughtered in no time, and a river of blood flooded the creature's womb.

The tank pulled up beside me. The trap door swung open and rat popped her head up. "What are you waiting for?" she screamed. "Throw the damn thing in the creature!"

Something clicked inside my brain. A voice started to speak to me. I quickly realized the voice belonged to the creature connected to my vital organs.

DON'T DETATCH, I heard it say.

I was mesmerized, caught in its lush vocal tones.

WE CAN TAKE OVER WHERE Kek HAS LEFT OFF. WE CAN GET NEW FOLLOWERS. YOU CAN BE THE VOICE OF THE NEW MAN. NO CTHULHU, NO Kek.... JUST YOU AND I... AND THE NEW WOR-SHIPERS...

She appeared before me. The young girl I was so in love with. The young girl who had lived next door to me and cared for her dead family. The young girl who was taken from me by Kyled. The young girl he had lied to, turned her into an in-human, all in the name of Kek.

DON'T DETATCH, she said as she moved closer to me, her strawberry-blonde strands sway-ing in the gentle breeze, the hem of her sundress swirling behind her. DON'T DETATCH.... I LOVE YOU TOO MUCH. THIS WORLD CAN BE OURS. WE CAN TAKE WHAT'S LEFT OF IT AND TURN IT INTO THE WORLD WE USED TO KNOW. WE CAN HAVE MANY CHILDREN, MANY FAMILIES.....

I turned to Rat and Miriam, who was scream-ing at me. I couldn't hear what they were saying, as they were being drowned out by the young girl's own beautiful sing-song vocals, which by now had been the voice of thousands interwoven together.

WE CAN HAVE THE WORLD, she was saying. IT'S OURS FOR THE TAKING. NO ONE CAN DETER OUR REASONINGS, OUR DECISIONS WILL WHOLLY BE OURS.... OUR DOGMA.... OUR BELIEFS.... WE WILL RULE *TOGETHER*... RULE TOGETHER...

TOGETHER...

OURS...

AS ONE...

One shot was fired. The bullet caught me in the temple. I felt immense pain swell as blood dribbled into my eyes. The young girl faded away and all I saw was toad head of Kek struggling to remove the creature from its chest. Tentacles dug deep into Kek's chest, removing its heart.

Kek burst into a mound of dishevelled yellow flesh and dissolved into a green liquid.

I heard Miriam sob, and in a hazy column of failing sight, I saw Rat comfort him.

"It's okay, Miriam," Rat said. "I know you loved him. But he was too weak to finish the job."

I thought about that, even if it hurt too much to think. Rat was right. In the end, I was too weak. I saw her and Miriam climb into the tank. "We've got to head to the Mid-West, Miriam,' Rat said. "No time to lose. Cthulhu is next to rid the world... ..maybe after that," Rat looked around and sighed. "We can help rebuild..."

I could feel life slowly drain from my ravaged body. A chemically enhanced vulture held my body down with his hands and fed off me, as the tank drove chaotically off into the dark of the night.

Mark Slade lives in Williamsburg, VA, U.S. with his wife and daughter and a Pomeranian who uses mind control on humans. In Sept. 2013 Horrified Press released his first book, a horror-fantasy-western, A SIX GUN AND THE QUEEN OF LIGHT. He is co-editor with Nathan Rowark of the horror magazine Nightmare illustrated, *which is in the spirit of EC Comics.*

THE IMPERIAL BANQUET

E. W. Farnsworth

The emperor and his retinue travelled in secret throughout the universe. The emperor's doubles observed random patterns to lure assassins and crowds of useful idiots. Of all threats, the emperor most feared his own family. Evidence of his plan to eliminate his relatives was kept out of the public's view. What the people did not know would not hurt them, or so they thought. The channels of open communication were filled with conspiracy theories and false news. Lately, the rumour of a great imperial banquet was spread. The source for the rumour was, as always, Kek, whose bloated, bloviating head appeared on everyone's display.

According to Kek, the senseless internecine killings were to be stopped by rational discussion over food. All the royals had agreed to attend in person in the Andorax System nearest the Pillars of Creation. Few could believe the promise of a truce. Most feared a trap, the aftermath of which would send the already evil empire into a death spiral worse than a black hole. The last such effort had led to a half-century bloodbath with a billion deaths. The only positive result was the elimination of many of the worst sort of beings. The blood suckers who remained had only survived because they were more ruthless than those who had perished.

Truth had departed the universe when Cthulhu and the Elders turned their backs and left. Their wisdom had held the reins of rule together for a while. Now nothing held, and no one could be trusted, least wise the Emperor and his rotten rabble. Humans, androids and artificial intelligences were nonplussed how to organize as a resistance. Technology had made thoughts transparent to imperial agents, who had the power to execute malefactors summarily. And how could a citizen recognize an agent? They were capable of taking any form and were so numerous in all the systems, they seemed to be everywhere at once.

Kek knew the aggregate views and played factions off against one another constantly. His reportage of the banquet made it seem as if the Emperor was deathly ill and needed to proclaim an heir. Only a royal who attended the banquet was to be deemed appointable. No one related to the imperial line, however remotely, could afford to be absent from the meal. Kek explained it thus: "Any royal not present will be deemed a rebel and, under attainder, will be hunted down and killed."

Viands from the far corners of the galaxies were shipped to Andorax for the feast. Aphrodisiacal fowl were shipped live so they could be slaughtered fresh and roasted. Flesh, eggs and tongues of rare birds were prepared with sauces laced with drugs, including those space pilots used for accelerated passage. Grains and nuts and breads composed of them were matched with liquors and wines in such plenty that entire solar systems might have been fed for Earth months. This in a time of universal famine, worthless currencies and savage cannibalism.

The emperor and his wives dined exclusively on the flesh of royals, freshly killed. They bred their own kindred and used their closest relatives as their tasters. Kek denied the rumours of the imperial cannibalism, but the practice was an open secret, the more to keep the people enthralled by the atrocious habits that spilled down from the top by example. Failing to maintain the distribution of food stocks, the empire encouraged its subjects as well as its slaves to eat each other though such practice was, naturally, illegal and subject to the death penalty.

Kek's image with its ghastly smile licked its lips in anticipation of the imperial banquet. He pledged he would be present to report every salient detail. He burped from satiety as he fleshed out lies about Cthulhu and the Elders agreeing to return to the feast as honoured guests. The lies kept the citizenry on edge with anticipation. They knew the great prevaricator could tell no sooth, but they had no alternative but to harbour hope of salvation. They did not banish Cthulhu. His vanishing was of his own accord, or so the imperial proclamations attested. Where in the cold, inhospitable reaches of deepest space could anyone last for long. Kek constantly reminded those who listened to his constant, blithering roar that self-murder was preferable to despair or to rebellion. The groans of captives punctuated Kek's broadcasts. The tortured faces of captured malefactors wrung the last forms of pity from the fickle crowds.

To Andorax would wend a multitude of trillions of soulless entities, drawn out of curiosity to witness the epic turning of the tide of rule. Glad they were that the emperor might be dying. Yet none could number any of his potential heirs as being quite as good as he was, though he was evil to the core. Kek reported the slow vivisection of the royals who came early to Andorax. He claimed the early arrivals had proved their perfidy by plotting to disrupt the festivities. The emperor was pictured devouring the bloody limbs of his dear cousins in the hope their blood would reverse his fatal condition.

Among those who arrived at the system

and remained alive were those who brought rich tribute in the form of rare universe metals and hosts of slaves. Some came from galaxies they had plundered and destroyed so they would be free to assume the imperial yoke without encumbrances. Their rapacious behaviours continued during their voyages. Reports of their rapine and defilements after their arrival only betokened their lineage and their special protection. Ordinary folk would be summarily killed for minor infractions or for trumped-up charges with no substance.

Princess Califrond was an early arrival who survived. Kek announced her coming with glee. Her deviousness was legendary. Her palace guards daily slew victims in ten thousands. She laughed at supplicants and lent her hand in the ritual slaughters of special personages. She once threatened Kek himself, and he boasted he was the only victim who had eluded her bloody tentacles. Confused by one of Kek's doubles, she had squeezed the green monster, only realizing her mistake when it flew into a trillion pieces laughing.

The emperor had whispered that it was high time for a woman to become supreme ruler of the universe. Yet his every move was to undercut females' power and eliminate them once they had bred and reared their broods. He deemed them no better than breeders for his table. Califrond was to be the primary taster for his feast, and her brood was to form the basis for the delicacies. She suspected the old ruler of treachery, but she had a counterplan with finesse. She thought she could trick the imperial trickster and turn his devices back upon himself. After all, he was rumoured to be dying. She wanted to be sure the rumour became fact.

Kek, in vengeance for her attempt to kill him, discovered her plot and informed the emperor, who decreed that, when the princess appeared in court to perform her ritual tasting, she should be seized and quartered as his appetizer. This Kek reported to the populace because he knew it would be disbelieved. Califrond believed him and seasoned her plot accordingly. She fashioned a double from one of her slaves. She used the code of death, not life, and made the taste of this creature irresistible.

The faux Califrond was duly seized and quartered. The emperor ate her greedily. Kek did likewise. Days later the emperor's bowels burned. Kek's broadcasts were subject to such horrid pain that his listeners laughed to think he was finally suffering as he had made many others do. The emperor raged and fumed in his diseased condition. He roared that Califrond had poisoned him. Now both the emperor and his universal messenger were languishing. The trillions processing to the feast now began rejoicing. Could it be that the horrible reign might be ending?

Now Andorax filled with royals and their retinues. Citizens flocked to be present at the historical event. Bellowing in pain, Kek railed at fate. The emperor was daily asked who would follow him. The emperor, having never experienced a killing disease that would not kill, delayed his judgment. Kek let fly every kind of rumour, pitting the assembled royals against each other. Open warfare ensued. Kin killed kin. Royals slaughtered their closest family members. Kek urged the killing to accelerate. The feast began in spite of the fact that the taster had not officiated. Califrond smiled when she heard the result.

Poison infused the bodies of all who partook of the feast. The emperor had suitable company since they all suffered from the same infernal malady. Kek took great delight in seeing others as wracked with pain as he was. The emperor was so pleased; he began to recover. Califrond visited her cousin when she heard he might survive.

"So, Princess, you formed a double, which I ate, and your double was poison."

"Your royal Highness, what did you expect? You planned to devour me."

The emperor held his belly. "Damned evil sprite!"

"Your reflection in a glass. Yet I'm not affected. I demand to be made empress by you."

"Never! You'll die in agony."

"Perhaps, but only after you. Thus far, the poison's effects have been superficial. As your stratagem prohibited me from partaking of your poisoned feast, I shall be the only royal to survive."

"In that case, I don't need to proclaim anything. You'll be made empress by your lineage. I have news, however. I have decreed that the new ruler shall have Kek as his or her consort."

She laughed. "Decrees of the dead are unenforceable."

The emperor pointed his finger at his cousin and said, "Kek, come forth!"

The great green figure came, making obeisance to his emperor. "You called, Majesty?"

The emperor gestured toward the princess. "She shall be empress, and you shall be her consort. What do you say to that?"

Kek's grimace of pain transformed into a mask of delight. "Your command makes me well again."

"Your first act will be to kill the empress and assume the rule of the universe yourself."

The princess drew her knife. She advanced on her cousin. Kek watched in fascination as she sliced the emperor's neck. He quickly grabbed her wrist and rammed the knife into her heart.

"So, Kek, it's time to make your proclamation. I am dying. The princess has been killed by you."

Kek smiled. "And all the other royals will die shortly. No one will gainsay my supremacy."

The emperor expired. His blood streamed into the pool where the princess's blood had flowed. Kek felt the burning poison inside him. He spoke to the multitudes as if the emperor was still alive. Knowing the magnetism of the royals, Kek pretended still to be their spokesman.

"The feast continues," he reported. "All should now partake of the feast by royal decree."

The multitudes ate at this universal communion. All who ate, perished. All who refrained from partaking, survived. So Kek became the de facto ruler of the universe, and chaos ensued. The great green lying head invaded the soulless souls of the living. All that Kek knew of cruelty, he magnified. All he knew of lying made his practiced falsehoods seem as good as truth. The general slaughter spread from the royals and their households into the general populations. The royals who did not attend the feast became agents provocateurs. The empire began to devour itself as Kek and chaos reigned supreme.

Hidden from view a fading fast from memory, Cthulhu and the Elders remained aloof. Misrule had finally become the polity of all galaxies. The infrastructures for all functions of state decayed—except for communication, which was controlled by the diseased and manic demigod Kek, whose croaking filled the void.

Only those beyond Kek's voice remained sane. Only those still capable of thought made a livelihood in spite of the disarray. Kek conveniently forgot the story of the emperor and the empress. His praetorian guards atomized the Andorax System so no sequel to the poisonous feast could be managed.

FASTEST GUN
IN THE GAMES

E. W. Farnsworth

Chris Harding achieved something his friends envied: he played video games for a living. Specifically, he provided reviews and quality assurance for quick-draw games designed around the popular mythology of the Old West. He was in such demand that he spent all his time gaming.

Recently, he tested a line of virtual reality rigs with guns and holsters fashioned to provide the gamer with a vivid, real-time experience, complete with scent supplements—for example, horse droppings, castile and gun oil. The brave new world of games promised environments in which the gamer could immerse himself or herself entirely. Typical of his audacity, Chris pushed the concepts to their limits.

Now he was permanently "in the zone." He no longer answered his cell phone or acknowledged text and email messages, even from his employers. He did not eat or drink or perform his normal bodily functions except in the games. Further, he became the most formidable opponent in massively multiplayer games. There he was known simply as The Kid, and he was the fastest gun ever known.

The Kid had studied the former fast-draws like William Bonney and Luke Short. He noticed their psychological nuances and made his own adaptations to their styles. Others saw themselves as acting out roles with a double vision —they were the spectators as well as the actors. Chris realized immersion in the gunfighter role was the key to success, but the truly great artists anticipated a fight and drove it to a satisfactory conclusion before the opponent was fully aware of what was happening.

In Dodge City, Kansas, the Kid became famous for taking on the young bucks and would-be killers, sometimes six at a time. Using his two-gun rig and changing his posture while firing both guns at the same time, he evaded bullets like a superhero and shot each man dead with a head-shot or a shot through the heart according to the rules of the game. He knew the delay times between the gamers' decisions to shoot and their reflexes with their trigger fingers. He reduced his reaction times to nearly zero. An example was the now-famous shootout at the Long Branch Saloon. At the time Luke Short was out of town, having been summoned by Wyatt Earp to be his faro dealer and bouncer in Tucson, Arizona. A group of young bucks rode into Dodge looking to take their chances with Luke. Unfortunately for them, the Kid was ready to take up the slack.

At the saloon bar, the rowdy young men drank whisky and jostled each other, upset their prey was absent. When the Kid rose from his seat at the table that sat in the centre of the floor, they sniggered and pointed. Chris, like Luke Short, was five-foot-five in his stockings and a little taller in his boots, but he was still shorter than any of the shooters. He waited with his hands above his holstered firearms until the laughter subsided. His eyes had a natural twitch, which signalled he was about to strike. The leader of the group made the mistake of touching the handle of his Colt. As fast as a viper, Chris drew both his guns and with three shots from each littered the floor with bodies. Chris sat back down at the table. He reloaded his guns and finished his drink before he made his way to the door, stepping over the bleeding bodies. No one challenged him until he reached the street where the sheriff and his deputy were running to discover why gunshots had been heard at high noon. The Kid climbed on his horse. He tipped his hat at the sheriff and rode out of town.

On the trail, the Kid picked fights with everyone who wore a gun or carried some other lethal weapon. In the gaming world, all men were natural enemies, and the law was impotent. So, the Kid would ride the range shooting a man with a Bowie knife or an Indian brave with his arrows or a man pretending to be Whip Wilson. Bodies littered the trail wherever he went, and they became the objects of interest for those who tracked him. As his legend grew, men hunted him in increasing numbers. Posing as outlaws or lawmen, in bands or a posse, his opponent fighters made it their role in the games to kill Chris Harding. He laughed. Knowing the play from the inside, he lured his foes into traps where he had the advantage. He ambushed many or rode right into their midst from behind to shoot them before they could get their rifles or pistols aimed properly. When he commandeered a wagon with a Gatling gun, he levelled a US Army company. He kept that wagon in a handy place, so he could deal with huge numbers.

Chris figured his greatest danger lay in female gunfighters. As gamers, they tended to have faster reflexes and more agile minds than the males. The Kid always knew when a female was disguised as a cowboy. She would be exercising her fingers constantly in preparation for a fight. She would also keep her eyes moving to find targets. The Kid did not know how many women he had outdrawn, but some of those had used stealth and indirection as tactics. One pretended to be wounded on the trail. She hoped to make the Kid drop his guard in pity. He saw through her ruse immediately and laid her low with a headshot. Another damsel, who feigned being in distress, elicited a witty ploy by which Chris grabbed a rattlesnake by the tail and flung it at her face. Her fear of the snake overcame her caution. She shot off the viper's head and earned a shot to the heart in return.

The only figures that the Kid truly feared were those who dwelled in the game perpetually. Those made the game an infinite study. Like him, the "immortals" knew the nuances the games' guru coders implanted into the software and firmware. They also knew the limitations of each weapon used. One such "lifer" used a high-powered Whitworth sniper rifle to ambush him on the trail. He was not sure what accident saved him from a fatal bullet, but the markswoman missed. She did not get a second chance to load and fire. The Kid rode directly at her in her rocky den. He laughed when she shrugged, but he splattered her brain across the cliff face behind her. He had the instinct to look for other targets. Sure enough, four other lifer women surrounded the place where the sniper had nested. Taking his victim's rifle and her pouch of ammunition, Chris Harding shot each of the other ambushers with headshots before he climbed back on his horse and continued riding the dangerous trail.

The Kid was a student of psychology. What occurred to him uniquely was the gaming world's equilibrium. By that he meant the unlikelihood of any super gamer remaining in the number one spot for long. The tendency for the other players to gang up on him or her made longevity unlikely. As a precaution against his being superannuated by a hail of hostile fire by too many opponents attacking at any one time, he kept on the move. His path was erratic. After he remained in Dodge City, he rode to Colorado. Then he traversed the Arizona Territory to Tucson on the way to the Mexican border. He stopped at the Oriental Saloon in Tucson just after the incident at the OK Corral. Wyatt Earp had departed, but Luke Short had departed long before. That did not mean the city was free of gunslingers looking to try their luck. As he rode into town, he shot three men dead whose horses blocked his path. Outside the Oriental Saloon, five young men and two young women made the fatal mistake of challenging the Kid to one-on-one combat. Feeling lucky, he said he accepted their challenges, if they faced him simultaneously.

Chris stepped over the bodies of those fallen challengers as he made his way to the saloon, but the danger was not over. At the bar stood four desperate men. The light was dim, but the Kid stepped out of the daylight at the entrance. That way his silhouette did not make him the perfect target. Using only one of his guns and fanning the hammer, he killed the four easily. Then he shot the barkeep, who had levelled a shotgun at his midriff. The hostesses moved toward him seductively, but he saw their malignant intent before they could bring out their concealed weapons. The floor was now covered with sawdust, dead bodies and brain splatterings. Calmly the Kid went to the bar where he poured himself a glass of whisky. He drank while he reloaded his guns. A gambler rose from the back table and walked to the bar. Chris did not waste the time to use his guns. Instead, he hurled a Bowie knife into the man's chest.

The Kid's gaming score was now the highest in the world. His name was blazoned for all players to see. A special chat room had been established for all who wanted to join in hunting him down. It was the most visited room, and the discussion indicated that the Kid would be targeted wherever he rode from Tucson. Monitoring the chat room gave Chris an equal chance of living or dying, but he took the risk of waiting in the Oriental until nightfall and riding south toward the border under cover of darkness.

While he waited, the Kid gunned down a dozen men and women who dared to enter the Oriental. Their bodies made it difficult for others to find their prey. In their fury at being hindered, his pursuers killed all the horses in front of the saloon, including his trusted stallion Ajax. If the gangs of shooters had wanted to enrage him, they accomplished their purpose. Still, he waited patiently until night fell.

Chris did not go out the front entrance. Instead, he went out the back way. He expected trouble, but he knew the darkness would play into his advantage. He used the body of the barkeep as a shield to draw the fire of those stationed out back. Those gunfighters' locations were evident from the fire from their guns. The Kid used both his guns to lay them low. He did not go around the saloon to the main street because he knew the horses were dead. He did not take a torch to light his way. Crawling under and behind the buildings, he made his way to the livery stable where live horses were available but under close guard.

Even more famous later than the thirty-second gunfight at the OK Corral was the one-sided shooting gallery of the Tucson livery stable. A dozen men and women died in fifty seconds of rapid fire. Others raced to the stable, but not in time to catch the Kid as he rode out of town to the south. The Kid used the landscape to mask his progress across the Mexican border. Now he had a makeshift posse of volunteers behind him and a plethora of gunfighters looking to kill him on sight in the bad lands just across the border. An advantage to the Kid was his knowledge that all he met south of the border were hostile. He did not have to discover a man's or a woman's intentions; he drew and fired as soon as he saw his prey. The string of bodies he left behind was a clear indication of his direction.

Chris Harding was heading to Mexico City with the Mexican Army massing to kill him before he got there. Relying on the natural confusion of military forces, the Kid exchanged clothing with a Mexican officer he had shot. The only things that made this disguise untenable were the speed of his draw and the bodies in his wake. Stories of his having killed an entire garrison of army troops enhanced his legend though they did not significantly raise his numerical score. He remained the number one player as the numbers of his opponents worked against his ultimate survival. Yet he wanted to survive, more to try his luck with the immortals than to prolong his life as a player.

The Kid used his nights to visit the chat rooms that addressed the immortals specifically. He noticed that Luke Short and Wyatt Earp were moving out of Dodge City to the south. His plan was therefore to travel east and north to cross the border again. This time he tried to avoid contact with his opposition. Only at the border did he resort to killing large numbers again. Now he changed clothing to look like a preacher though he still wore his twin six-guns. He moved from town to town preaching the gospel as he saw it and delivering men and women to their Maker. His message, gleaned from all he had learned as a gamer was increasingly clear: a gamer could achieve a kind of immortality, for a while, but eventually fall in a blaze of glory. The more he preached this message, the more it occurred to him that his having entered the gaming life forever was a kind of death to the ordinary world. In fact, he wondered out loud whether he could leave the game if only to re-establish contact with his own soul.

Though Chris Harding earnestly tried to escape his game to test his theory, he could not do so. He killed whomever he met easily on his way to his destiny as the greatest gamer, yet he suspected he was no longer of the living and that he had died when he left his parent's living room that last time. This insight gave his quest a kind of quiet desperation. His aim was to encounter and challenge the immortal figures one by one, so he could satisfy his own view of himself as the greatest of all time.

His greatest test was, of course, to draw against Luke Short. The man had married a woman named Hattie, who had the same name as his mother. He was rumoured to be ill, but that might have been a ruse. The Kid met Short in a small café in Albuquerque. The Kid was the faster draw against the game's factotum for the famous quick-draw artist. The Kid laughed as he rode west to find Wyatt Earp. "In the context of the game, what does immortal really mean?" he asked himself.

The Kid continued to kill the immortals. His reputation now was equivalent to a gaming god. The points he gained for slaying the greats of all time made him unapproachable. His petty single killings of lesser beings meant nothing to him. His speed remained consistent, and he was at the top of his form. Fools still challenged him, usually in groups. All failed to win against his lightning draw. He became accustomed to preaching over the people he had just slain. His message had altered somewhat because of his success against the immortals.

"What is immortality when even the so-called immortals return to the dust wherefrom they came?" he said over the body of Wyatt Earp's factotum. And over Annie Oakley's crumpled body, he amplified his lesson: "Here lies the greatest female shooter of all times. Yet I have laid her low. Such is an emblem of the transitory nature of fame. If you are swelled with pride, you could make the mistake of lowering your guard and letting lesser beings gun you down." Finally, when he had shot the game version of Billy the Kid, he intoned, "Thus fall the great. And William Bonney is now less than nothing. I am not proud, for pride shall have its fall."

Townsfolk in the Old West games gossiped about the supremacy of Chris Harding. The only detractions were born out of jealousy. Since the Kid had only killed figures in a game, they reasoned he might not have been fast enough to out draw the real, historical figures. This criticism rankled the Kid, but he could nothing to refute their claims. He rationalized the game conquests as the only accurate measure of greatness in the quick-draw competition of the present. He issued a challenge in every chat room listing the parameters that would grant a challenger the right to stand against him face-to-face in a shootout the old-fashioned way in the street at ten paces. Few could qualify, but many made the false claim that they had done so. Setting up shop in Dodge City, the Kid entertained the best of those who challenged him.

The local graveyard quickly filled. The challengers kept coming since with a single killing, they fancied they could claim all the Kid's fabled merit points. For a while, the winner would be top dog among gunfighters. Yet none could prevail against Chris Harding. Finally, a gunfighter and one of the immortals too, issued a challenge that sorely stressed the Kid. It came from John Wesley Hardin, the Classical scholar and gunfighter who never had lost a fight. His challenge differed from all others.

"Chris Harding, I challenge you to a shoot-out where you live. I won't come to your game-world Dodge City. I'll meet you instead at your home in Camden, New Jersey, known as an armpit of the universe. I'll knock on your door and insist that you come outside and draw in the street in the cold light of day. If I win, I'll take all your points and your status in the games. If I lose, you'll have done something no other gamer has done. You would have beaten an immortal OUTSIDE the game environment. What do you say to this?"

The Kid was impressed by the immortal's challenge. He knew it must be answered, yet it took him a long time composing a reply.

"I know, challenger, that you died long ago in

the real world. Yet you claim to be able to enter the street on which my home is situated. I am confident you will fail to make the transition. I have tried the same with no good effect. Go ahead and roust me from my virtual gear to receive your justly deserved second death. If you cannot do that, I'll meet you in the street outside the Long Branch Saloon in Dodge City where you'll become yet another immortal to fall in the gaming world. I anticipate your answer for, either way, you will lose, and I'll gain status from defeating you."

Weeks passed before John Wesley Hardin replied.

"You are a bloviating bastard and charlatan!" the reply began. "I've been to your home. Your parents informed me you were found dead in your VR gear and were subsequently buried in the local cemetery. I therefore claim that I have won in my encounter in the real world. I shall not meet you in Dodge City, for you do not exist except in your gaming form. That I despise and condemn. Fie on you. Surrender your points to me, or there will be dire consequences for you." He attached to his post an image of the death certificate and the headstone at the cemetery.

The Kid laughed at this challenge, which he thought idle and manufactured. He returned, "Do your worst, whoever you are! If you do not appear outside the Long Branch Saloon within the next seven days, I'll assume you've been a fraud and imposter."

The Kid waited the requisite seven days. The figure who posed as John Wesley Hardin never appeared. Still, Chris Harding had trouble assessing what his challenge meant. On the one hand, the Kid knew from personal experience he could not exit the gaming world and re-enter the real world from which he had come. On the other hand, the figure had provided evidence that his mortal self had perished.

He thought, "I am caught in a form of limbo between life and death, my gaming self being an intermediary state of being."

As if reading his mind, Hardin texted, "You are in a medial position, from which you cannot escape except by your death in the gaming world. I stand ready to assist in your deliverance. When you are ready, just let me know."

The Kid went on a killing spree unlike anything the gaming world had ever known. He challenged everyone he met and terminated the others since they were flawed, and he was perfect by the rules of the game. On day, he admitted to himself, "I grow tired of the endless killings. I long for my release and transformation."

That afternoon, John Wesley Hardin finally appeared in the street outside the Long Branch Saloon. Hardin called in a loud female voice, "I know you are ready to meet your destiny. Come out and face me."

The Kid walked out of the saloon into the street. He faced the figure who called himself John

Wesley Hardin, but the figure looked like Calamity Jane.

"Hello, Kid. I'm sorry it must be a female figure who will bring you low. Your time is short, and I was the best the game could manage. Whether you draw or not, I'm going to end your misery this day."

The Kid drew, but she was much faster than he. Three bullets tore through his head and heart. He was dead before he hit the ground. Onlookers stripped the dead body of the Kid's legendary guns. The game automatically assigned Jane the points formerly earned by the Kid. Chris Harding became a dim memory while Calamity Jane took on the role of supreme fast-draw gamer. The body of the Kid was buried in the same graveyard as housed his victims.

What happened to the soul of the Kid was—and is—a mystery. All that remains is the game, which continues.

WAY TOO GOOD TO BE TRUE

E. W. Farnsworth

Even superheroines have pasts, and some secretly harbour deep and lingering feelings for significant others who have had profound effects on their lives. Such was the case for The Intrepid Lady, whose past caught up with her when she was impelled to rescue a former schoolmate. He had gotten into trouble by his own devices and desperately needed her aid.

Before she became The Intrepid Lady, Emily had nursed a crush on Howard Dexter from the time they were both teenagers in the same class for "very exceptional students" at Hyram Poynter Middle School in Keystone, Nebraska. Over the years, the pair had remained in touch by corresponding—and sometimes by meeting when he was passing through her city on one of his many business trips to catch up over a quick Dutch-treat meal.

Emily therefore had kept abreast of her friend's inspired though often hare-brained software development schemes. His one redeeming talent was his prowess as a computer programmer, a talent which gave her some common ground with him professionally. They had never been lovers, and that was good for their brother-sister relationship. Their long absences from each other were also healthy since their friendship never became stale from over-familiarity.

In fact, Emily had not heard from Howard for well over a year, but she figured she was not her brother's keeper. Busy with her unusual superhuman works as The Intrepid Lady, she was startled to receive belatedly a long and troubling text message from Howard via social media.

The text had evidently been caught in her spam folder, which she had only by chance inspected prior to deleting its entire contents. The substance of Dexter's message was that he had been approached online by a total stranger with an international business offer that was "way too good to be true." Emily rolled her eyes as she reviewed his version of the terms of the scammer's deal.

Emily found it hard to believe her friend had fallen for one of the oldest tricks on the Internet. A risk taker with a yen to make a killing on every undertaking, Dexter had answered an unsolicited email from a man pretending to be a banker from the African country Benin with a problem that could only be solved by Dexter in person in Cotonou, the capital of his country.

The chief difference between this hoax solicitation and other run-of-the-mill scams of the same ilk was the instant deposit of $250,000 into Dexter's own private bank account, which Dexter had verified before he booked his flight to Benin. Also included in the fine print of the "sweet" deal was an unsecured personal loan of the balance of ten million US dollars after the initial amount had been factored in. By accepting the initial $250K in his account, all terms of the arrangement, including repayment stipulations, kicked in.

The Intrepid Lady would have been wholly unaware of Dexter's departure and subsequent disappearance except as an afterthought just before his exit, the man had sent his girlfriend a text describing his luck and bragging that he would return from his journey a very rich man.

Alarmed that the young man's text was now over a year old, Emily dropped everything and wasted no time finding her way to the fabled Ear of Africa. There, disguised as The Intrepid Lady under the pseudonym Miss Rosalie DuPreet, she made her devious way to the semi-secret compound northwest of Cotonou where Umdugu's victims, termed his "guests," were housed until their "debt" was paid. His game was clearly a kidnapping-and-ransom racket,

The Benin businessman Banda Umdugu stood almost seven feet tall. He was regally handsome, muscular as a body builder and suave. He might have fit right in on Wall Street as an investment banker—and, for a while, he did just that.

The Intrepid Lady had researched the man's background thoroughly. Court records indicated that Umdugu had spent as much time on Wall Street as he subsequently had done in the US prison system for crimes such as extortion, fraud and embezzlement. Now his brilliantly white teeth glistened as he greeted "Miss Rosalie Du-Preet."

Impressed by her good looks, hourglass figure, excellent grooming and attractive smile, he gave the woman a "Cook's Tour" of his spacious facility and extensive grounds. He was unaware of her identity though his secretary was frantically scouring the Internet for details—in vain—while they surveyed first his offices in the main building and then his sprawling jungle compound, which was surrounded by a twelve-foot chain-link fence topped by razor wire. Both persons were exhibiting the effects of the sweltering heat as sweat first stained and then soaked through their clothing.

The Intrepid Lady was both impressed and appalled by what she saw. Here, within this gated enclave tucked deep in the jungle, Mr. Umdugu kept his prisoners on subsistence rations in a virtual prison with scant sanitation, where his guests waited for friends, relatives or business associates to pay exorbitant ransoms for their release. Flies, mosquitos and a host of other winged, biting insects plagued the inhabitants while one-hundred-percent relative humidity made breathing difficult even for those who did not suffer from respiratory allergies.

Dense overhead triple-canopy foliage blocked any vestige of a breeze, and daily afternoon rain drenched the area and left standing pools of water, raw sewage and miasmal mist, perfect for breeding all manner of diseases.

With each laboured breath, The Intrepid Lady inhaled putrid African jungle smells, redolent of urine, rotting fruit and faeces. She forced herself not to gag while nodding to Umdugu's fluent recitation of platitudes about his sinister trade. He eyed her with unabashed lechery as she made a handsome figure in her khaki jungle outfit and wide-brimmed safari hat.

The sole proprietor, apparently unaffected by his steamy surroundings, said, "Every one of my guests is here waiting for his or her assignees to repay the loans they have taken from my bank. In most cases, the amounts owed me are well over ten-million-US dollars." He had moved near enough to touch her when she swatted his hand away as it swung toward her bottom. While she deflected his blow, she deftly stepped aside so he would no longer remain in her personal space. He smiled as if she were just being coy with him, as if he would possess her if he were persistent.

The Intrepid Lady clarified her position in no uncertain terms: "Keep your hands to yourself, and we'll be fine. I've counted over one-hundred guests thus far, so your potential harvest is significant, to say the least. I'm impressed that anyone could run a scam with such egregious scope and terms in a time when transparency could reveal the underlying corruption and bring an end to it at any time."

The large man shook his head and laughed out loud. "Of course, my business is profitable! After all, I am a successful businessman." He winked at her. "My accountants tell me how much time a debtor can spend here before I turn him or her over to the national authorities where, after due process, they will enter one of our national penal colonies.

"The advantage of my compound is the possibility of a way out." He let that thought sink in. Then he continued, "I presume you wish to help one of my guests settle his or her obligations so as to be free to depart? I urge you to get right to the point, or I'll have you forcibly removed from the premises and turned over to the Benin authorities."

She nodded. "Let's take the example of that young man who was hunched over his computer, working on the software program adjacent to your office. How much debt would he need to repay you to become free?"

The scam artist arched his right brow and

rubbed his goatee with two well-manicured fingers. He thought for a moment as if calculating the answer to her question. When he thought enough drama had been created, he said, "That man, Mr. Howard Dexter, is a special case for me on account of his software development skills. He has almost completed a social media program that will change the world. He will not be easy to replace.

"I'll have to sacrifice resources to get anyone remotely as capable as he. Therefore, for him I will require repayment of his ten-million-US-dollar loan and any accrued interest—plus an additional ten million dollars to pay for his replacement."

His eyes narrowed and focused on hers. He seemed glad that she had not flinched at the amounts he quoted. She, in turn, could tell by the greed in his eyes that he was racing to think up a way to increase the victim's ransom.

She asked, "Do you require a bank transfer for the funds?"

He scowled. "No! There will be no bank transfers. I don't trust electronics. I may be old fashioned, but I much prefer cash," he said, his unctuous smile becoming a malicious leer. "Let me have my accountant make out the invoice for Mr. Howard Dexter's release. You can consider my terms and arrange for the cash transfer through others while you remain in the compound. Or, alternatively, you can depart after our discussions and return within two-to-four days with the cash to settle the account. I can allow you to talk with my guest now in a private room if you like."

"Yes, Mr. Umdugu, I'd like that. But for our discussions, I want us to have absolute privacy."

He led her outside to a grass hut in a jungle clearing. Colourful parrots perched on the hut's roof preening and spreading their wings in display. A huge man, armed with a machete and dressed only in a loincloth, stood by the door of the diminutive building. He looked just like an Egyptian caryatid guarding the entrance of a temple.

Inside the dark interior space, Umdugu gestured for Miss DuPreet to sit on a cushion by a low table in the centre of the single room. He lit the candle on the table with what looked like a solid gold; then departed.

By candlelight, The Intrepid Lady noticed the walls of the hut were lined with closed terrariums containing venomous snakes and poisonous spiders. Each glass enclosure was fitted with a clear vial large enough to transfer the living creature when necessary.

Separately, coiled around a wooden post in the far corner of the room was a huge python that eyed her with a frozen stare. She could not tell immediately that the fearsome serpent was alive. She watched in fascination until the reptile's head moved slightly. Emily was now convinced it was alive—unless it was a cunning robot.

Soon Mr. Umdugu returned with Howard Dexter, who sat on a cushion at the table opposite her. Looking as pleased as if he had performed a miracle, the businessman proudly placed an invoice for twenty million dollars "and change" on the table facing her.

"Miss, I am happy to present your invoice." Turning to the young man, he said, "Howard, I'll be sorry to see you leave me. You've done excellent work." When Dexter gave no acknowledgement, Umdugu shrugged and said, "I'll permit you two to discuss the delicate matter of payment in private for one hour. Then I'll return so we can make specific arrangements." He laughed as he stood and walked to admire one of the poisonous spiders crawl into its vial. After rubbing his finger across the glass to excite the spider, he departed the hut.

Dexter said, "Hi Emily. I'm frankly surprised you managed to penetrate the defences that surround this compound. That probably means you're now as much a prisoner as I am." He smiled, and the faux smile evaporated as her eyes bored into his. He winced under her lingering gaze. "It's good of you to come, but I have little faith that you or anyone else can extricate me from my unfortunate situation. I feel like such a fool!"

"Howard, you have certainly proved your folly this time. I suspect Mr. Umdugu is listening to every word we're saying, so I'll make this short and sweet." She lowered her voice to a whisper and leaned towards him. "Hang onto your hat as I'm going to get you out of this hellish place."

Dexter turned pale and blurted out, "How do you propose to do that, my friend? Surely, you don't have twenty million dollars in cash! Even if you did, I'd never have the means to repay you." He seemed perplexed and hurt, as if she had taunted him with an impossible hope.

She shook her head as she might with a doubting child. Dexter had seen that look on her face when they were in school together.

"Have I ever lied to you, Howard?"

"No, you have not. That's one of the endearing things about you, Emily: you never lie."

"There you have it! I'm going to perform the miracle my way—by bypassing the giant ape-man at the door to this hut, by walking through the forest of hanging serpents and jumping spiders, and by evading the lions' preserve in the plain. I only require that you not involve any of your fellow guests in our secret venture."

"Emily, I'm reluctant *not* to help the other victims. I've only survived my year here by exchanging favours with many other victims. I owe them more than I can ever repay."

"I'm sorry, Howard. I can only take one person out of here, and you are going to be that one individual. Once we are both free, we can get the authorities involved to shut this abominable institution down for ever. Are you coming with me *alone*, or not coming at all? If you aren't coming, I'll just retrace my steps and go home."

She let the thought hang between them. Her

eyes shifted to the door. She noticed a female peccary nose her way into the hut and hustle for the dark corner where the snake was coiled on the post.

Dexter seemed oblivious to the drama that was going to unfold at the back of the shadowy space. Looking at his hands, he answered, "You give me no choice. I must agree to do as you say."

She nodded as the snake dropped from its perch on top of the peccary. Its coils rapidly enfolded the porcine beast in its looping, constricting body while the victim struggled vainly to become free. Emily breathed out slowly, relieved that, unlike the peccary, Dexter had chosen wisely.

"Good! I'll bargain to return in three days with the cash ransom. Will you pack everything you'll need and be ready to move in two days?"

He nodded. "Yes, Emily, I'll be ready. You'll see that I have precious few belongings."

She smiled as she examined him closely. When she was finished, she said, "To prepare for our journey, you must sleep, eat and drink as much as possible during the next forty-eight hours."

"There's not much food or water to be had. And sleep is nearly impossible on account of the racket the guards keep going all night. My only peace is getting 'into the zone' with my software." He slapped a mosquito that had landed on his arm. A trail of blood trickled down through the river of sweat on his forearm. He licked the blood and pressed the mosquito bite hard with his thumb to stop further bleeding. Of course, he could not stop the streaming sweat.

"I know these people are not likely to be allowing you to go online. Still, I'll bet—despite them—you've been able to make a list of automated bank accounts that your boss controls."

"You're right about that. I can provide you the list of Umdugu's accounts with their passwords and some other interesting accounts as well. To your implied question: I have not gone online since I arrived here. There's simply no way for us guests to do that. That's ironical since the success of the program I have been writing depends on gauging its net worthiness."

"Your list of accounts and passwords should be sufficient to my purpose."

"Arrange for Umdugu to let me describe my program to you at my workstation. While I tell you about my exploits, I'll slip you a thumb drive containing a file loaded with all you'll need. Gosh, Emily, it's great seeing you again. You're a jewel just for giving me hope! I'll never forget you for this."

She rolled her eyes. "Save the praise for later, once you're on the ship heading out to sea beyond the twelve-mile limit on the first leg of your trip home to the USA. Right now I want you to focus entirely on getting ready for your escape. You look emaciated and dehydrated. To travel, you'll have to rehydrate and get some meat on your bones."

Until Umdugu's return, Howard and Emily caught up on their activities since their last meeting. She could not say anything about her alternate identity as The Intrepid Lady. Instead, she told him about what she did to make a living in the city. In turn, he talked about how he had survived in the jungle compound for twelve long months.

"I've often been hungry and thirsty. Unlike many others, I have not been feverish. I've witnessed many attempts to escape. Umdugu's men, all tough and ruthless members of the same warlike tribe, have been effective, albeit soulless, guardians. Apprehended escapees have been stripped naked and beaten senseless with a strap in the clearing. Not many guests have been freed on account of payment of their ransom; one $10M person a month keeps the government paid. Several guests have died one way or another on account of the jungle."

"Can you think of any important contacts this place has with the world outside?"

He thought for a moment before he said, "Once a month, the Benin government sends a uniformed representative in a green Rolls Royce to collect taxes due—ten million in cash packed in a suitcase."

"When will the tax man come next?"

Howard said, "He'll come in four days." As if punctuating this remark, the snake hugged its gasping victim, and broke its bones, which snapped with the sound of firecrackers. The Intrepid Lady was not thinking of "nature red in tooth and claw" but of her fledgling escape plan.

"That makes my appearance timely since Umdugu will need the cash for your ransom to pay his monthly tax."

As if on cue, the businessman ducked through the door. He sat on the third cushion by the table. Umdugu glanced in the dark corner where the snake was now attempting to swallow the still-living peccary whole, head first. He chuckled at the spectacle. The Intrepid Lady saw the look denoting creature recognition. The scam artist was, indeed, like the python, and his victims were like the helpless peccary caught in the snake's powerful coils.

"What have we decided to do about your payment?" As the giant asked this, he drew a knife from a sheath concealed inside his light coat. He used the tip of the blade to clean under his fingernails. Turning his hand one way and another, he waited for the young woman's answer. The knife may have been the symbol of his power over them, but for The Intrepid Lady it was a reminder that this kidnapper and extortionist deserved the death he was likely going to get before they were truly free.

Miss DuPreet said, "You'll have your ransom in three days. In the meantime in prospect of your receiving the cash, I want Mr. Dexter to have as much food and fresh water as he desires. I also want him housed in this hut with minimal intrusions, so he can sleep. What do you say to that?"

"I grow tired of perpetually talking terms." He yawned for effect but stopped when he saw the fire in the woman's eyes. He watched a drop of sweat cascade down her brow and cheek. He ran his tongue around his lips, squinted and yelled out, "Mbamba!"

When Mbamba the guard entered the interior, Umdugu told him, "Fetch bread, fruit and vegetables with a pitcher of clean water. Place everything on this table."

Soon the table was full of bread, oranges, bananas, pineapples and other fruits, which Dexter ate greedily while Emily and Umdugu continued their negotiations.

"Miss DuPreet, I'll make this simple. From you I need twenty million US dollars in cash in three days. Otherwise Mr. Dexter and you shall remain in this compound as my guests, with release costs increasing daily until all amounts owing are paid in full. Do you understand me?"

"Yes, Mr. Umdugu, I'm afraid I do understand you. I will present to you twenty million US dollars in cash in two suitcases. After you have given us a receipt for that amount, you will then allow this man and me to depart your compound unmolested. Further, *in advance* you will prepare the government paperwork necessary for Mr. Dexter's free departure from Benin."

He stopped paring his fingers for a moment

and looked up. "So you want a *laissez passer* too. Don't you trust me? In any case, I'm sure you're aware of the costs of your additional request."

"I'm aware that ten million of the twenty I give you will go to 'taxes.' Without that money in hand, you'll not be able to stay in good graces with your government."

He raised his right eyebrow, and his eyes dilated. "You are surprisingly well informed."

She shook her head. "I warn you. If you change any of the terms of our agreement, I assure you that you'll suffer consequences you won't like."

At this threat, he laughed so loud the guard rushed into the hut to be sure everything was all right. Umdugu waved the hulk away with one hand and turned to face her again. "Is there anything else?"

"Yes. I'd like a personal tour of the work area where Mr. Dexter has been busy with his computer, so I can see why his freedom should cost ten million dollars more than the amount for repayment of his loan."

Umdugu rose from his cushion and led the man and woman back to the office next to his in the main building. He looked at one and then the other as if trying to imagine how good a couple they made. "I'll leave you alone to discuss Mr. Dexter's software development effort while I tend to some urgent matters with my secretary. When I return, it will be decision time for you."

Alone with Emily, Dexter rubbed his mouse over his mouse pad, so his computer display came to life. He said, "My job has been to design a computer dating game that eventually will assist lonely hearts to connect to their soul mates. If you like, I can walk you through my user interface."

"That won't be necessary, Howard. The last thing I want is to become involved with you via your computerized match-making program. Say, I suppose you could reconstruct what you've created here once we return to civilization?"

Dexter looked at his computer monitor, wrinkled his brow and said, "Most probably, yes. Anyway, I can take a copy of the program with me. Technically, the copyright is mine as its creator. Of course, code modifications and testing will be necessary as the software package I'm forced to use here is hopelessly antiquated—and not as yet connected to any network. Good Lord, it's hot even with the building's air conditioner going full blast."

Dexter picked up a damp cloth and mopped his sweaty face.

She was unfazed. "Then you aren't likely to have wasted a year in this hell hole for nothing?"

He smiled weakly. "Except that here in the jungle I have not had the chance to talk with *you* occasionally, not till now anyway."

She avoided his pleading eyes by looking aside at his shabby office. The stench of mildew and human excrement was almost overpowering her olfactory senses. "I'm glad I finally managed to find you. Once you're out of here, though, I want you to promise me never to take such a terrible risk again."

He winced and nodded. "I promise, I think." He picked up a thumb drive. After inserting it into the USB port of his computer, he downloaded a file to it. Emily stuck out her hand, and he placed the drive in it. Gratified, she closed her fist and stuck sit in her purse where she put the thumb into a special compartment made especially for such precious things.

As an afterthought, he mentioned, "By the way, the file is encrypted. To open and decrypt the text, all you need is the name of the school where we first met in lowercase, with no space between the words. That propitious meeting seems as if it happened an eon ago. I can't tell you how many times during the last year I've thought we were intended to be together."

The Intrepid Lady hardened herself to give them both courage. She straightened her posture, so she stood almost at attention. "While I'm gone, be good and keep faith. Don't pick any fights. Remember that I'll be back for you soon, and you'll be going home."

Umdugu barged into the room unannounced. "Miss DuPreet, what have you decided?"

"I'm leaving this compound at once. I'll return in two days with your cash."

He stood at his full height and grinned

broadly. Unctuously, he said, "I know you'll be back on time because your friend will not be treated well if you are late."

"Mr. Umdugu, my friend had better be treated well right up to the time we are out of here. Or else . . ."

His eyes narrowed as he leaned forward menacingly. "Or else what, Miss DuPreet?"

"Do you remember the peccary that was eaten by the snake in the hut?"

"I remember that incident quite vividly. That snake was an inspiration to me—and it should serve as a caution to you."

She stepped forward suddenly and startled him. "If you hurt my friend, your death will be like the peccary's, only more painful. Now I'll leave you. I remember how I came into this building. I'll let myself out now." With that threat, she turned and walked down the peeling linoleum floor of the main hall to the exit. Outside, her cab was still waiting to return her to the tourist section of Cotonou, where she had booked a suite at one of the finest hotels in the city, the Golden Tulip Le Diplomate. She had planned that the suite would be her command centre for her operation until she returned to the hellish compound.

In all of Cotonou, there may have only been a dozen bottles of the same fine Chablis that Emily drank that night. She had a long night of hacking on the Internet ahead of her, but the stakes were as high as she had ever bargained for. She ordered an ice bucket with two bottles of the white wine from room service and got straight to work with her laptop. Having checked the Internet connection upon her arrival, she knew she could connect in all the right places to do what needed doing to accomplish her mission.

Emily's first task was to use the encrypted file on the thumb drive that Dexter had prepared for her. She had no trouble downloading and decrypting the file with the password "hyrampoynter." With the account information on the resulting clear text, she transferred thirty million US dollars from a mix of Mr. Umdugu's sundry bank accounts to a pristine offshore account in the Cayman Islands she had opened years ago on a whim but never used till now.

After a few more sips of white wine and a hot bath, she was ready for the next phase of her hacking exploit. Fortuitously, Dexter had included the number and password for the Benin National Treasury account, whose contents would be more than enough for her needs.

Emily relieved the Treasury account of one billion USD by transferring that sum from that account to Mr. Umdugu's personal checking account. The Intrepid Lady was sure that the legitimate national and international banking interests would detect this transfer, and many sleuths would be very interested in such a large denomination transfer.

While the computer was executing her transfer, she thought, "Tracking money laundering is still more of an art than a science. Nevertheless, to quote the American Senator Everett Dirksen, who allegedly said, 'A billion here, a billion there, pretty soon you're talking real money.' I sincerely hope the bankers will be diverted from fixing on my own machinations by this huge transfer implicating Mr. Umdugu."

Having done what was necessary, Emily decided to take the advice she had given to Dexter and get some rest. She reasoned she had plenty to do the next morning, and she needed to be sharp.

The next morning, Emily, still using her pseudonym Rosalie DuPreet, dressed well and took a cab to the Bank of Africa, where she ordered the transfer of thirty million US dollars from her virgin Cayman Islands account to a new temporary account from which she withdrew the entire sum as cash in three suitcases, each containing ten million US dollars. Inevitably, she was picked up outside the bank by a uniformed man in a green Rolls Royce and whisked to an office of the personal secretary to the President of Benin.

Situated in a chair across the immaculate desk of the self-important potentate, who had served them both Darjeeling tea, she heard, "Miss DuPreet, the president has taken a personal interest in your safety while you are visiting Benin. He has placed me at your service." The tall, thin, thirty-something man sat upright, his upper lip with the tiny moustache twitching. Emily thought he liked to show off his long manicured and moisturized hands.

She responded, "That's very kindly of him. Judging from the upscale, contemporary look and feel of your capital city, I shouldn't have thought that I was in any significant danger of being robbed by common criminals. Nevertheless, how do you suggest you can help with my security?"

"Miss DuPreet, as we in authority know, unscrupulous parties would be delighted to relieve you of the cash in your three suitcases at their earliest opportunity."

She nodded pertly and asked, "What specific services can you provide?"

The bright young man said, "We guarantee absolute portal-to-portal security, provided that none of the funds you are carrying cross any borders of this country. And, of course, there will be no troublesome inspections by my government or any other powerful interests."

"That sounds like a most attractive offer, coming as it does from the very top." She read no sign in his face showing he was conscious of her ironical tone. "May I ask how much your services will cost me?"

"Yes, Miss DuPreet; our normal fee is one third."

She cocked her head to one side. "That does seem a little steep, don't you think?"

The man's smile transformed into a look of grave concern. "Miss DuPreet, we will be involving the highest levels of the Benin military and security services on your behalf. I assure you that every penny of our fee will be well spent. If you leave one of your bags with me, I will take care of *all* the little details. You won't have to worry about anything."

Before she could answer, he had pressed a tiny red button on his desk.

A highly decorated, greying soldier appeared at the door. "At your service, Sir!"

"Colonel Mikado, please meet Miss Rosalie DuPreet."

"Miss DuPreet, I am charmed to meet you." He bowed so low that The Intrepid Lady had difficulty suppressing a smile.

The president's secretary said, "Colonel, you will protect this woman and her parcels with your life. Do whatever she asks of you. At the end of her stay in our country, you are to return to attend to your former duties. Until then, your duty is to serve this woman exclusively."

The colonel snapped to attention, clicked the heels of his spotless black shoes and saluted his superior with a loud "Yes, Sir!"

The president's personal secretary nodded toward the bags, two of which the colonel hefted. The secretary himself spirited away the third suitcase through a side door opening on the president's office, just as The Intrepid Lady knew he would.

The Intrepid Lady said, "Colonel, today my

business has been concluded. Please escort me to my hotel—the Golden Tulip. There I'll brief you on what you must do for me tomorrow."

Back in her suite over glasses of freshly squeezed orange juice, Emily instructed the colonel what he was to do. She was very specific about the resources, the vehicles, the weapons and the tactics. She was clearly in command, and the colonel told her he "would do whatever was necessary to make her stay in his country a success." He appointed two armed and uniformed soldiers to guard her suite from the outside. She heard the colonel order the guards to accompany her wherever she wanted to go both tonight and tomorrow.

It was therefore with a full military escort of two Humvees full of soldiers that Miss Rosalie Du-Preet arrived the next morning in the green Rolls Royce at the offices of Mr. Umdugu. The colonel assisted her out of the car and personally carried the two suitcases of cash into the building.

Coincidentally, when they arrived at his office, representatives of the Benin Treasury were present to escort Mr. Umdugu to the presidential residence for intimate discussions of one billion missing US dollars, presumed to have been transferred illegally from the National Treasury account to Mr. Umdugu's private checking account overnight.

Before Umdugu was permitted to depart, Colonel Mikado helped Miss DuPreet deliver the two suitcases of cash and receive the receipt she had been promised, together with the *laissez passer* from the Government for safe passage from the port of Benin for both her and her friend Mr. Howard Dexter. Mr. Umdugu's secretary counted the cash twice, and his accountant deposited the cash in the company's walk-in safe.

The Intrepid Lady and the colonel then immediately walked to the hut where Dexter was to have been housed while she was gone, but her friend was no longer present there. The snake was still on the floor, with its bulge indicating the meal of one peccary that was slowly passing through its alimentary canal. The terrariums were unmolested.

The colonel's men conducted a thorough search of the compound, but their search revealed nothing. Miss DuPreet was not pleased.

She seethed, "Colonel, I demand that Mr. Dexter be produced immediately. I order you hold Mr. Umdugu here until this matter has been resolved."

The colonel nervously shifted from one foot to the other and explained, "Miss DuPreet, I cannot hold up the national inquiry any further. We must approach the president's secretary to resolve any remaining issues."

Miss DuPreet was no longer listening to the befuddled, blustering factotum to whom she had been entrusted. She marched back to the hut and extracted one of the venomous button spiders from its terrarium in the hut. She went directly to confront Mr. Umdugu with the creature in a vial. She presented the vial containing the deadly spider, so the scammer could see it clearly. The big man flinched and trembled in fear as he recognized the same arachnid he had admired earlier in the hut.

The Intrepid Lady said, "I will ask you for the last time: Where is Mr. Howard Dexter now? If you don't give me a satisfactory answer, I'll release this spider and let it bite you. You know it will bite, and you'll sicken and most likely die from its poison.

Everyone stepped back from the hostile encounter. Miss DuPreet advanced a step towards Mr. Umdugu, her hand with the vial extended threateningly. The man was sweating profusely and shaking from fear. He leaned away from the cursed spider. His eyes did not leave the vial.

Umdugu stammered, "My guards took him out of the compound and into the jungle just after the Treasury people arrived. Right now I don't know precisely where they are, but they departed from the north exit gate to the rear of the compound. There is only one thin path to follow through the jungle. You will find them on that path. Please don't release that spider. It is very deadly."

Miss DuPreet told the colonel, "I am going to trade you this spider for your sidearm and two extra clips of ammunition. I'll find my friend and meet you again in the port area at the steamer we have chartered for the departure. When I return your arm and ammunition, I will expect to receive that spider in our exchange." She made the trade and raced off in the direction Umdugu had indicated.

It was nightfall before The Intrepid Lady caught up with the three-person guard and her friend. Howard Dexter, supported by one guard on each side, seemed to be weak and vacillating. Mbamba, the chief guard, made the mistake of resisting by threatening Dexter with his machete. The Intrepid Lady shot the strong man in the hand, causing him to drop his weapon before he fled back down the trail towards the compound. She appropriated the machete and made sure that Dexter was well enough to continue, provided that the two remaining guards kept him upright. With the weapons, she motioned for the guards to keep to their path going north and not to think of going back south to the compound. As they proceeded, the jungle darkness closed around them and high-pitched insect and amphibian sounds filled the air.

All night they followed the narrow footpath to the north. They heard scuffling of predators and prey to both sides of their path. At one point, the forest opened into a grassy meadow where prides of lions paraded and hunted in the dark. Their path continued through the meadow. When the flat, grassy field terminated, and they had no trouble picking up the path through jungle again.

They emerged from the jungle at dawn to find a logging road running east-and-west. Emily now allowed the two guards to return to their compound through the jungle. Happy to be free to go, they fled. They left Dexter sitting on the ground by the roadside.

Emily meanwhile turned east and flagged down the first truck heading in that direction. An empty logging truck stopped to pick her up. She importuned the driver to help her lift Dexter into the cab. She asked the driver to drop them off at the first intersection of any road that ran south to the coast.

By now Dexter was feverish and subject to delirium. Emily did what she could to comfort him, but she knew the best course of action was to return to her hotel suite where they could remain in relative safety until he was well enough to travel.

Three transfers later, they hitched their final ride to the Golden Tulip Hotel where they stayed in her suite while she nursed him for three days. Finally, his fever broke in a cold sweat that passed over his entire body. Emily ordered food via room service daily to give him strength. She encouraged him to use the exercise and sauna facilities of the hotel to restore his health.

Feeling somewhat domestic and practical, Emily bought them both new clothes in the shopping district, and, dressed in their new outfits on the upscale streets of Cotonou, they looked like an ideal, young tourists, even newlyweds. This was not a pleasant metaphor for Emily, but she figured that it suited their improvised cover.

The local newspapers covered the arrest of Mr. Umdugu for the computer theft of one billion US dollars from the Benin government. The funds had been recovered from the man's personal accounts, but his business license was revoked, and his business summarily closed pending the results of his public trial.

Meanwhile, Umdugu protested his innocence, pleading that he had absolutely no technical knowledge of how to transfer funds on the Internet. He claimed that he had been robbed and not the other way around. Details of his statements led the authorities to the man's secret bank accounts and many other criminal lines of inquiry. Nothing in the public media indicated that The Intrepid Lady or her friend had been implicated or even mentioned.

"Emily, I think it's strange that Umdugu could have been party to computer crimes when he was a flagrant ignoramus about technology. I believe he must have been framed by someone who has not yet been identified."

The Intrepid Lady said, "Hmm." She did not want to enlighten her friend about her subtle moves. She had no idea where the information might lead. She said, "I'm glad the man's kidnapping and ransom operation has been shut down. I'm also glad you were not named as having escaped or evaded the man's clutches. If the papers we were given are valid, we should have no trouble leaving this accursed nation. Still, we should watch our backs."

Dexter laughed. "What should we be looking for? I don't think Umdugu is in any position to do us harm at this point."

"One thing I always liked about you, Howard, was your innocence."

He huffed, "I suppose you're going to tell me some conspiracy theory about Umdugu's connection to the Benin government. I grant you, his payments of ten million dollars each month imply a close relationship, but there's nothing in the newspapers about those payments yet."

She frowned. "I suspect those payments never will be made public. You might be onto something about that, but you're not on the right track."

He looked at the ceiling and shook his head. "Tell me what you think."

"I think the government just lost an income stream of ten million dollars a month. The president has also been taking a cut from being the middle man in cash transactions. What do you think will happen to the $1-billion the government found in Umdugu's personal account?"

"Are you implying the operation was too valuable to the government to shut down?"

"Yes, I am. Sure, the compound you inhabited was shut down, but Umdugu told me about secret penal colonies run by the government. I think the operations never stopped. All the guests at the old compound have been transferred to one or more government facilities with far worse conditions than you experienced."

Dexter thought about this for a while. Then he stood and paced the room. "So, Emily, what do we do about the situation?"

She picked up the souvenir machete that she had shot out of Mbamba's hand. She examined its blade and checked its balance by adjusting its position in her hand.

"Emily, my dear, did you hear me? Stop playing with that useless blade and answer me. Tell me what we are going to do about the injustices we have uncovered?"

The Intrepid Lady did not answer for five full minutes. Her mind was racing with the possibilities. "Howard, do you have computer work you might do in this room while you recover? You can use my laptop if you like."

"You know I do. Give me your password so I can work."

"You already know the password: "hyram-poynter.""

He smiled. "Kindred minds…"

"Whatever. I may want to change it after this trip." She was beginning to think she wanted nothing further to connect herself to this man and his history.

"What will you be doing in the mean time?"

"I'll be shopping. Do you need anything while I'm about it?"

"The rain is torrential. You'd better dress for it—and take an umbrella." Dexter was already fixated on programming on her computer. "And thanks, but I don't need anything. Just be careful out there."

The Intrepid Lady changed into her jungle gear. Selecting an umbrella, she left the suite and took a cab to the presidential palace to meet the president's personal secretary.

She learned it was one thing to meet the secretary in a business suit with suitcases full of cash on a sunny day and quite another thing to meet him in safari kit wielding a machete and an umbrella in a downpour. Miss DuPreet was politely informed that she should wait by the service entrance for her reception.

She stood behind a spreading tree at the rear of the palace and watched the service entrance as a limo and a police vehicle screeched to a halt in the rising flood. From the building came a huge man with a bandaged right hand. He carried a revolver in his left hand and spoke through the window of the limo before he went back inside. The limo pulled out and circled the building before heading back where it came from. The police vehicle remained for a few minutes aimlessly. Then it too left the area.

The Intrepid Lady returned to her hotel suite to change clothing. Decked out in her business attire, she went to the Apple Store Cotonou. There she arranged with the manager to surf the Net privately for a large bribe.

Once connected to the Internet, The Intrepid Lady visited the bank accounts she had come to know from her previous sojourn. She transferred another billion dollars from the Treasury account to the personal account she had established under her pseudonym at the African Bank. She liberated another billion dollars by transferring it to Umdugu's personal account. A third billion she transferred to the account for Apple Store Cotonou.

The Intrepid Lady then composed a long anonymous letter to the editor of *La Nation.* The letter was an encomium on the Benin president's largesse specifically for repatriating individuals who had been kidnapped and held for ransom by Mr. Umdugu at his illegal premises northwest of Cotonou. She continued in this vein to praise the man's judicious expenditure of one billion dollars of Treasury funds to support computer literacy throughout the nation via Apple. Finally, she commended the man for starting a fund to clean up and reform the penal colonies of Benin.

Stepping out of the Apple Store, she hailed a cab and returned to her suite.

Dexter heard her enter. "I'm glad you're back. Do you know what has happened?"

"Why, no, Howard. Tell me."

"While you've been out shopping, Benin's largest newspaper has received an anonymous letter trumpeting the president for reforming the nation's penal colony system. Further, he has pledged to return to their countries of origin all hostages held at Umdugu's compound. I can hardly believe it."

She shook her head. "Well, I wouldn't believe it until I saw signs those things were actually happening. I sincerely hope they will happen. Old Dahomey once had a good reputation for being a stable democracy and an example for African nations."

"I think we should celebrate."

"So call room service and surprise me."

Dexter did just that. The two enjoyed listening to the national news while eating the best meal they had shared since Emily's arrival. She saw that the young man's health was surely improving.

While they enjoyed themselves, investigative reporters were evidently busy. The news outlets were full of emerging facts and innuendoes. Knowledge of the penal colonies was a scandal reaching back to the days of African independence from colonialism. The press was demanding a full list of the hostages who had been kidnapped by Mr. Umdugu. The greatest clamour was about enormous sums of money.

Touching his champagne glass to hers, Howard said, "One way or another, Mr. Umdugu is going to be destroyed by the notoriety he has received."

"I'll believe it when I hear it from the judicial process. The president will mull over the situation and choose the best course of action for him, personally. We'll be lucky to see one tenth of the found money going to reform the penal institutions of this country." She drank her champagne and strained to hear what was being said about the funds that had found their way to the Apple Store Cotonou. "The news hounds have done well," Emily thought, "but so far they have not discovered what they termed, 'the Apple connection'."

Dexter said, "Say, I didn't know Apple had planted a store here in Benin."

"It's a small world, Howard. It's a wonder the dirty dealings of Mr. Umdugu have not seen their day of reckoning before now."

"Didn't you say we would be leaving Benin tomorrow, weather permitting."

"Yes, and the morning is supposed to be sunny. From the tenor of the news, we may be getting out of Dodge just in time."

So it was that one week after they had made their escape from Umdugu's compound, Emily checked them out of the Golden Tulip Hotel. They made their way side-by-side to the port area of the capital city where their ocean transport was still awaiting their arrival. Their next challenge was to get past the army security unit that was keeping the steamer under strict surveillance. The Intrepid Lady knew the surveillance was meant for intercepting them.

Fortunately, the commander of the army's security forces was Colonel Mikado, the same man whose charge it was to see to their safe departure from Benin. The man seemed to have forgotten his mission, however, and he tried to extort from the young man and woman a "bonus payment" of a suitcase of cash for himself prior to their boarding the steamer.

Dexter passed out on the pier just before The Intrepid Lady executed her deft escape manoeuvres, which included returning the colonel's gun and two ammunition clips in exchange for the vial with the button spider in it.

The Intrepid Lady threatened to release the spider. She watched the soldiers scatter. Meanwhile she told the ship's captain to shove off and get underway as she commandeered a deck mate to help her pull her friend over the gangway. The steamer pulled away from the pier and headed for open water. Looking back at the pier, The Intrepid Lady saw a Jeep pull up and an excited man with a bandaged hand gesticulating wildly. Colonel Mikado was arguing with the man. His Benin army troops watched helplessly as the vessel departed. The Intrepid Lady wondered how they might regroup without knowing what to do about the spider. She and the deck hand managed to get Dexter belowdecks and into a cot below.

Howard Dexter only revived hours later, on a cot in the innermost cabin of the steamer where

Emily, no longer disguised as Miss DuPreet, heard him curse his luck for "losing" the fortune he had been promised by Umdugu at the outset. His memory of what had happened was either non-existent or skewed. For example, he was puzzled about how Emily had accomplished his escape, which was now complete on account of their being outside the twelve-mile limit..

"Don't get me wrong. I am eternally grateful for what you've done for me. I don't know how I deserve your many kindnesses. I want you to itemize all your expenses, so I can one day repay you."

Emily told him. "It had nothing to do with deserving anything. You were just lucky this time —but in future, you had better not depend on having such help as I've given you again. It was only by chance that I discovered your text message, and I just happened to be free at the time to locate and assist you. As for repayment, I shall submit my expenses and my hourly fee for the interval. I expect your dating program will eventually be lucrative, so you can delay paying me until your revenues from that venture arrive."

The young man shook his dead, apparently little wiser than he had been before his departure from the USA. Emily was glad to have rescued Dexter, but she knew she had lost whatever respect she had harboured for the young man over the years.

Emily saw Howard Dexter off on the first

flight of his long itinerary back to Cleveland, Ohio. By then, they both knew this was their last good-bye.

Emily decided not to accompany Howard home, but instead she flew to Ouagadougou, the capital of Burkina Faso. There she intended to visit a famous witch doctor to share notes on magic spells.

The Intrepid Lady knew she would be not be welcome to return to Benin under any name. She also knew that magic, like communications software, worked at great distances with no need of human presence on the receiving side. She felt strongly that Mr. Umdugu deserved much more of a penalty than a free pass for what he had done as a scammer. His shady kidnapping and ransom business had been foreclosed by *force majeure*, but it still might continue under the rubric of the Benin penal system. The Intrepid Lady wanted the bad man excluded from any business whatsoever for the rest of his life. Magic was going to help, or so she thought.

As for Howard Dexter, she wished him no harm. He was merely oblivious to the evils by which he was surrounded. She recalled the good times they had shared. She wondered why she had not seen the man for what he really was until she had witnessed him under duress in a trial for his life. "If I had not found his text message and rescued him, he likely would have perished. That rescue, fortunately, does not obligate me further. When I think what a mistake it would have been to marry him, I shudder. Again, I have confirmed that celibacy is the only path for me. Besides, Howard is married to his software. It seems ironical to me that a man who has no stake to hold in interpersonal relationships should write code to bring people together forever by means of the Internet. So much the better for them, I suppose. It's not my cup of tea."

RETURN OF THE CREATURE FROM THE BLACK ROCK RESERVOIR

E. W. Farnsworth

Daniel Strong and Carrie Anderson met one late summer near midnight at the Riparian Preserve near the public library at the intersection of Greenfield and Guadalupe Streets in Gilbert, Arizona. Star-crossed lovers with their match opposed by their career paths and by both their families' prejudices, they came together against the odds in out-of-the-way places where prying eyes would not discover their furtive, romantic liaison. Since few visited the preserve after dark, the lovers felt safe. Almost.

The young man and woman walked hand-in hand by the water with a billion stars shining in the desert heavens.

"I understand why we're meeting here, Daniel. No one will find us here, but this place gives me the creeps."

"Carrie, we've got nothing to worry about. The danger passed when that SEAL team took out the monster. The beast is dead, so relax."

"I shudder to think about that giant, slimy creature." She shivered and hunched her shoulders. Instinctively, she edged closer to him.

He put his arm around her shoulder. The cooling desert air was listless. Carrie leaned into him for protection. They both looked out on the still, black water of the preserve.

As they walked, she thought about how little time remained before he would depart for basic training in Chicago and she would go north to Flagstaff to finish her nursing degree.

"Life isn't fair," she said, stamping her foot. "Tomorrow, you'll depart for the navy and I'll be all alone again."

A splash interrupted their reverie. "That must have been something huge." Carrie snuggled close to Daniel. Her eyes tried to find the source of the splash in the darkness.

"Don't be thinking about the monster. That splash could have resulted from any number of causes."

"Just the same," she said, "let's reverse course. It may seem silly to you, but we shouldn't tempt fate."

He obliged her. He remained closer to the water than she as they returned to their parked vehicle. In the starlight, he saw something round and shiny protruding from the water's edge. He pulled out his cellphone and activated its pen light to examine the object. Carrie froze and waited while he continued.

"I don't have a good feeling about this," she mumbled, but he may not have heard her.

Daniel was apparently fascinated by what he saw. The light went back and forth over the ground. He walked forward while his girlfriend stood moaning, her arms crossed over her chest.

"What's that?" she said pointing at the sand leading toward the water's edge.

The pen light followed her gesture. "It's a dark slick of something."

"Is it blood?"

"I don't think so. At least, it's not likely. Calm down. You have an over-active imagination."

"Be careful, Daniel!"

As he approached the bump, he whispered over his shoulder. His voice had an edge. "Carrie. Don't ask any questions. Just run to the car as fast as you can. After you get in, close the windows and lock up. I'll be there as soon as possible."

"What have you found?"

"No more questions. Get moving. When you're inside the car, dial 911. Say we've found a body."

"A dead body?"

"Yes. Now move!"

Alarmed, Carrie did as she was told. She ran to the parking lot and climbed into Daniel's Saab. She rolled up the windows and dialled 911. Carrie could not see Daniel through the windshield. She texted, "IMOK in the car. I dialled 911. Police are coming. RUOK?"

Daniel texted back, "IMOK. Please remain in the car no matter what happens."

Waiting for the police, Carrie was scared for Daniel—and super vigilant. She dimmed her cellphone screen and strained to see what was happening though the windshield, but all she saw were silhouettes of palm trees arching over the preserve like silent guardians. Her mind was crowded with possibilities. *Is Daniel safe? Has he encountered a monster?* She was interrupted by Daniel's knocking on the window.

He slipped into his car and locked the door.

"Well, what did you find?"

"It looked like a human body, only it was skinned and headless."

"That's scary. Is the body still there?"

"That's the trouble. As I approached, something pulled it under the surface. The arms waved behind it. Then it submerged and vanished."

"What could have done that?"

"I don't know. I know I saw something. But I can't prove what I saw. Everything happened too fast for me to take a cellphone picture."

"Well, I saw the bump too, but not with any definition."

The police arrived with lights flashing and sirens blaring.

A female officer approached the Saab with a flashlight in her hand. Daniel rolled down his window.

"Did you call 911?" she asked.

Carrie answered, "Yes, officer. I called. We were walking along the preserve when we saw something—a bump on the edge of the water."

Daniel continued, "When I approached it, something dragged it into deeper water and took it under. It disappeared."

"Can you tell what the object was?"

He said, "I thought it was a headless corpse. In the light of my cell phone, it appeared to be all bloody. As it was pulled under water, its arms waved back and forth. Then it went below the surface."

The policewoman told the couple to remain in their vehicle while she investigated. They saw her flashlight scan the area as she walked along the shore. She stopped near the place where Carrie had seen the slick running down to the water. After running her flashlight back and forth over the slick, she came back to the Saab.

"Whatever you saw is gone. On my camcorder, I have a recording of what you said you saw. I only need your identification to link to your statement." Daniel and Carrie gave the officer their Arizona drivers' licenses.

"What do you think we saw, officer?" Carrie asked.

"Ma'am, I have no idea. Absent physical evidence, I'd only be guessing. We'll probably have a dredging crew out here the first thing in the morning to try to find the corpse. Thank you for calling. We'll take it from here. I don't think we'll need anything further from you, but if we do, we'll call."

After the police car departed, Daniel turned to Carrie, "Well, we don't know much beyond what we saw. We'll have to trust that law enforcement will discover the truth."

"I have goose bumps. I'm just glad we're safe. I wouldn't want either of us to end up skinned and headless in this place—or anywhere else. Speaking of elsewhere, why don't we drive up South Mountain, just for the view. It's unlikely we'll be in danger there."

The lovers enjoyed a few more hours together that night. The next morning, while the couple went their separate ways, the police dredged the area of the preserve nearest the slick that ran down the shore. The slick was human blood, and a grappling hook caught a skinned, headless female corpse.

The on-scene commander documented the

Jane Doe as a murder victim. The remains were subjected to detailed forensic analysis. Assigned to the case, Officer Bekkah Roundel recognized a pattern that might apply—the creature from the Black Rock Reservoir, but she remained silent by direction of her chief.

"It's not good public policy to mention the possibility of another prehistoric predator on the loose in the preserve. The former creature you encountered was slain: that was the end of the story. That case is now considered closed."

Officer Roundel nonetheless phoned Lance Curlow, the SEAL Team commander who had partnered with her to defeat the first creature. She told him in confidence what she had learned. He gave her good advice: "Bekkah, until you have hard evidence, you won't be able to obtain the resources we'll need to do what's necessary in this new case. When you have the evidence, call me again. I'll fly to Phoenix, if necessary on my own dime using accrued leave. Together, we'll devise a plan."

"That's sensible advice, Lance, but I feel in my bones we're going to enter a world of hurt while we delay."

Officer Roundel arranged to remain the lead officer on the new Jane Doe case. That was easy since no one else on the force wanted to handle it. An excellent researcher who liked working with the police forensics team, she discovered in a matter of hours that the corpse belonged to a woman named Hazel Groundswell, a colourful figure in

Phoenix media circles whose license plate was B2YAGA. Groundswell had been reported missing by her live-in friend Dawn Larsen two days before her mutilated torso was found at the preserve. Larsen claimed that Groundswell had been hunting a menacing phenomenon that dwelled in the preserve.

She told Roundel, "Hazel was obsessed. She saw an extremely tall, webbed thing on two occasions stalking the periphery of the Riparian Preserve. The figure was easily twice as tall as any man Hazel had known. She wanted to commune with the beast alone. So she parked at the library every night and walked along the water."

Groundswell's car with Arizona license plate B2YAGA was located in the library parking lot and impounded as evidence. DNA signatures of samples from the woman's car and the nameless corpse matched. Police had no evidence to make a murder case though for a short while Dawn Larsen was a person of interest. The case was subsequently reclassified from murder to misadventure under the name Hazel Groundswell. Still, the police chief would not permit any public speculation about a monster lurking in the preserve.

Once Larsen was excluded as a suspect in her friend's death, she showed Officer Roundel Groundswell's chapbooks documenting her thoughts about the creature. Included among records in the chapbooks were clippings from the violent sequence of events that led to the demise of the menace that had terrorized all Phoenicians for months. Also included were notes from dozens of interviews she had conducted. Groundswell's own drawings of the creature were strikingly like the photographs and images in documentary films of the creature from the Black Rock Reservoir. There was no mistaking that Groundswell's monster was similar to the lone creature everyone had presumed to be killed. Roundel was intrigued by the woman's speculations about the number of monsters that probably remained after the index creature had been killed.

With her evidence pointing toward the likelihood that Groundswell had found the monster for which she was searching, Roundel phoned her SEAL team contact again. This time, she brooked no delay. "Lance, we have a clear and present danger right now. You must come to Phoenix to review the latest evidence I've found."

In an abundance of caution, Commander Lance Curlow flew to Phoenix secretly to review the bidding with his former accomplice, Officer Bekkah Roundel. In conversations with the SEAL Team commander in a suite in the Camelback Hilton, Roundel argued, "The only possible cause of Groundswell's death could be the ravages of a creature like the last one we encountered and overcame."

Over club sodas with ice, she showed Curlow the evidence she had amassed, including the chapbooks of Hazel Groundswell. He also carefully reviewed the recording of the young couple's encounter with the remains.

"Daniel and Carrie were lucky that night, Bekkah," Lance said nodding.

"Do you agree that the torso's disappearance below the water of the preserve could only have been the result of the creature taking possession of its food?"

"That makes sense. Nothing else does."

"Lance, let's cut right to the chase. Do you think I have enough to make the case for reopening the idea of a man-eating creature being at large again in Greater Phoenix?"

"You may not be able to break through your chief's reluctance, but I have enough to engage my superiors—if you're willing to entrust all your evidence to me."

She saw no alternative but to hand over the evidence in the hope the Special Forces could be enlisted in the hunt for the new creature. Without a hideous attack by the monster, the police department would stonewall any discussion of the new menace.

The SEAL team commander flew back to his base with the evidence. He was determined to convince his chain of command to engage immediately.

Meanwhile, Bekkah Roundel continued to search for evidence of the creature while she opened her mind to all the possibilities. She took a week of vacation to consult with a few local experts and to rethink how the former successful hunt had been orchestrated.

We had a long line of gruesome deaths before we mounted the operation to eliminate the creature whose first appearance was in the Black Rock Reservoir, deep under Phoenix. At the time, we calculated that the creature was a loner though that assumption may have been erroneous.

I am now facing evidence suggesting the first creature was not a singleton. That makes good biological sense, but it also implies that many creatures might have survived, and not only in the Black Rock Reservoir.

We brought the first creature up from the reservoir to the preserve. Did the creature's escape open a new gateway for the whole species? If it did not, was there an existing conduit between the two watery domains allowing free passage from one to the other? The creature was not only superior by natural adaptation, but it was also preternaturally intelligent, malevolently so.

The more Roundel thought through the problem, the more she became convinced that a conduit must exist between the reservoir and the preserve and that the original creature must have exploited it to liberate at least one other specimen of its species.

She concluded: *Now the monster is no longer contained underground in the reservoir. It can emerge and hunt on the surface whenever it desires.*

Roundel informally discussed the creature

with an ethnologist at Arizona State University. The professor showed Bekkah numerous Native-American images of creatures devouring humans. The Southwestern examples alone raised the hairs on Roundel's arms. "As you can see, Officer Roundel, the crude drawings feature monsters twice the size of the men and women they are devouring. These creatures are embedded in the psyches of the indigenous peoples of Arizona."

A marine biologist professor at the same university informed Bekkah, "Some female amphibians are now known to reproduce without having male counterparts." He additionally thought, "It's highly unlikely that a monster would produce only one offspring. My professional opinion is that, whether a reptile or an amphibian, your monster probably spawns dozens of offspring. The subsequent spread of the offspring assures geographical distribution as well as a plenitude of food. If too many specimens inhabit any one place, they would rapidly deplete available animals they would need as sustenance."

Two nearly simultaneous events proved that Roundel's growing fears were justified.

First, Dawn Larsen, not content to have her friend die a horrible death and dismemberment, followed in Groundswell's footsteps to hunt the monster on her own. As in the case of her friend, the huntress became the hunted. Her last communication was a 911 call warning that she was being stalked by an enormous web-limbed creature, which emerged from the preserve at midnight.

The next day after her call, Larsen's body was found mutilated beyond easy recognition and skinned by the side of the preserve.

The police chief was intransigent. Even after Roundel importuned him to activate a formal hunt for the creature, her chief was adamant about maintaining silence. At his insistence, news reporters had factual stories spiked by their editors. Misinformation was distributed about the possible presence of serial killers in Greater Phoenix. By this strategy, a general panic was contained, but such containment came at the expense of the truth.

Second, four fishermen disappeared in the Black Rock Reservoir.

It was impossible to contain news of the disappearance of four fishermen who motored into the reservoir, only to disappear without trace. One of the fishermen happened to be a major philanthropist, beloved throughout Arizona. The man's family pressed the mayor and chief of police for answers. He, in turn, caved in to political pressure and summoned Officer Roundel to his office.

"I'm assigning you to the case of the mysterious disappearance of four fishermen in the Black Rock Reservoir. You are to focus entirely on this case. I want you to use any resources you can muster to get to the bottom of this mystery."

Officer Roundel nodded. "Chief, if I discover that a monster caused the disappearance of the four men, what then?"

"Officer, I sincerely doubt you'll arrive at that conclusion, but we'll apply the principle of Occam's Razor in any case: the simplest explanation that satisfied all the facts, will prevail. Do whatever you need to do. I need answers within the week."

Roundel did not hesitate to phone her SEAL Team commander even though he was already supposed to be working to convince his leadership to engage.

"I confess, Bekkah, I could not convince my chain of command to commit resources before now, but your new assignment may convince my hierarchy to change their collective minds."

"Lance, we have exactly seven days to solve the mystery. You know what we needed last time —you and I were seated before a campfire to lure the beast into a trap. Let's work together again, starting now."

The SEAL Team arrived at Sky Harbour the next morning. Lance vectored half his team to the preserve; Curlow tasked the remainder to use rubber boats to scour the reservoir with their special sonar gear.

Deep underground in the reservoir, the Special Forces made quick progress with their side-looking sonar and diving equipment. They located on the bottom the detached motor of the fishing boat that had carried the four fishermen. Along the shore nearby the wreck, they found remains of a recent camp and fresh, bloody human body parts. Hearing of their successful find, the commander warned his men, "Take extreme measures to protect yourselves. Consider you are under attack from the wiliest, ruthless enemy you've ever encountered." He remembered how he had lost an entire team to one of these monsters the last time around. He did not want history to repeat itself.

On the surface near the preserve, SEAL Commander Curlow and Officer Roundel camped on the shore and built a campfire to attract the creature just as they had done on their last adventure. They positioned the other members of the team in a semicircle surrounding their position with instructions to fire at will at any attacking monsters.

There was a difference this time. The commotion made by the military presence naturally caught the attention of investigative reporters, who had felt insulted and deprived of a good story. One intrepid and reckless reporter, Agnes Dolgrath, decided to work embedded with the preserve team even though she had been warned by Curlow that such actions were unwise. Dolgrath's fool-heartiness was, ironically, just the right prescription to lure the creature out of the water.

The monster moved like lightning from the water to the shore and snapped the spunky reporter's body in half with three gigantic bites. The Special Forces soldiers did not hesitate to slay the creature before it could re-enter the water.

The prospect of documenting the death of Dolgrath and execution of the weird creature brought the entire Arizona media community to the preserve. When the vans of media equipment arrived, all that remained to be filmed were the two halves of Dolgrath's bloody corpse and the huge lifeless body of the reptilian creature. The heroic combatants had rapidly redeployed underground to reinforce their comrades.

The mayor and chief of police were left to their own devices to preen and boast about the slaying of the monster. They made a fatal decision to deny prior knowledge of the resurgence of the creature that had terrorized Sun Valley. They also neglected to mention that the battle against the monsters had gone underground because at least one additional creature dwelled in the subterranean Black Rock Reservoir.

"We're saddened to announce the death of Agnes Dolgrath, reporter, who gave her life to discover the truth about the presence of a new monster in the Riparian Preserve. Fortunately, law enforcement successfully killed the monster, but not before it had cruelly taken Dolgrath's life. Phoenix was imperilled, but now, thanks to a reporter's heroic sacrifice and efficient law enforcement, the menace is dead and gone for good."

"Mayor, is it true that monsters may have been involved in the disappearance of the four fishermen in the Black Rock Reservoir?"

"Nothing could be further from the truth. Where do you people get your information? The only monster we know about is lying there dead on the ground."

"Will you tell us about any involvement in these events of the SEAL Team that landed at Sky Harbour this afternoon?"

"The SEAL Team is coincidentally here on a routine training exercise. I don't see any Special Forces soldiers here. Do you?"

"I have a question for the chief of police." An earnest, carrot-top reporter said this.

The mayor nodded and surrendered the makeshift podium to his chief law enforcement officer.

"Sir, was the dead creature also responsible for the demise of Ms. Hazel Groundswell?"

The chief shook his head. "My, what vivid imaginations you reporters have tonight. We are focusing now on the sad death of one reporter and the happy extinction of one monster. Emergency personnel are dealing with the aftermath. There's no sense trying to claim that every mysterious death must have been caused by man-eating monsters."

"Mayor, one last question. If other monsters *are* found tonight either here in the Riparian Preserve or down in the Black Rock Reservoir, can you assure the people of Phoenix they are, indeed, safe."

"Let's not incite panic, young man! Did we

mention anything about other monsters besides this dead specimen? This monster is dead as you can plainly see. That's all for tonight."

The media frenzy calmed after the mayor's solemn pronouncements. Images of the monster and file photos of Ms. Dolgrath made the national news.

Deep under the city the Special Forces and one intrepid female police officer, Bekkah Roundel, worked hard to unravel the rest of the skein of data linking the pieces of the story of the creatures. Those fighters were now combating an unknown number of monsters on the shore of the subterranean reservoir. The media had no presence in this arena; only those involved in the fight were aware of the odds—and the consequences.

"Commander Curlow, you surely do know how to show a lady a good time," the police officer joked as they navigated their passage through the darkness to the far side of the reservoir.

"I'm just glad I didn't lose any men fighting that berserk reptile on the surface."

"If I'm not wrong, we'll need every one of your soldiers for this next phase."

"Put me in the picture, Bekkah. What are we facing?"

"It's unclear, but consider what it would take to guarantee the survival of any species for millennia. *Homo sapiens* is thought to have been decimated from time to time. We were reduced to as few as a couple of thousand humans at one stage.

Now we threaten the globe with our billions. Yet we might have been extinguished. As for these monsters, we have fictional evidence they existed in the early Christian era, as witness the Old English poem *Beowulf*. And here in the Southwest are images of such monsters eating humans for millennia. We know the latest evolution of this beast is over fourteen feet tall."

"Miracle of evolution or not, I'm afraid I'll have to opt for exterminating the whole monster species—the sooner the better."

"You asked for my assessment. I think these monsters have the same idea about us as we have about them. They want to destroy us all. However many there are, they're going to be in the fight of their lives, and the result will be their survival or extinction."

She hesitated to let her thought sink in.

"Look ahead. Isn't that the campfire of the contingent we sent below earlier?"

Commander Curlow focused on the flickering flames on the shore. "It could be. I don't see any activity around the fire. I surely hope my men haven't gone to sleep."

As the black rubber boat pushed toward the shore, the grim reality of the situation became clear. Bodies of soldiers lay in pieces around the fire as if they had formed a square and died to the last man against overwhelming odds.

"Good grief!" Curlow cried. "Those men were the flower of my command. Can it be that they all were killed? How many monsters would it have taken to overwhelm their firepower?"

Only one SEAL remained alive to tell the tale. He was critically wounded, but he managed to report—and Officer Roundel used her cell-phone to record his message.

"Commander, they came from every side, quick as a flash. They absorbed fire that would have finished most humans, yet they survived. I don't think we killed any of the monsters."

"How many of them were there, son?"

"Three dozen, maybe four." The man could no longer stand the pain. His back arched, and he died in his commander's arms.

Curlow gently closed the dead man's eyes with two fingers. He looked at the policewoman incredulous. "Forty monsters? We do have a problem. And *none* were killed!"

"Commander, what do you suggest we do now? We have the same number of SEALs left as we sent here below. If we stand and fight without reinforcements, we'll be slaughtered like the others."

"I agree. We need reinforcements, and we need them now before we engage."

Roundel said, "The square formation won't work against the monsters. You'll also need more powerful weapons than your men possessed here. On the surface at the preserve, it took all the firepower of half your team to destroy just one of the monsters."

"You're right, Bekkah. We must retreat before we're all killed. Men, gather your comrades' dog tags, weapons and ammunition and break up so we can take as much as possible using all the fast boats we have."

The SEALs worked rapidly, treating the fallen respectfully and the ground as sacred.

Curlow told Roundel, "We SEALs don't leave our dead behind. In this case, though, we'll come back for their bodies when we bring the reinforcements."

The unit's second-in-command said, "Commander, we'll be leaving a feast for the monsters. Think of what we're doing as buying time to reach the surface and escape."

The commander nodded at the young soldier's wisdom. He chambered a round and served as overwatch as his men worked fast so they could leave.

As the living cut through the reservoir the shortest way to the entrance, the policewoman looked back to see the monsters emerge from the water. Around the waning campfire, they were devouring the slain. None bothered to pursue the escaping troops. Perhaps they figured they had enough food for this night.

The commander and the policewoman felt glad the survivors made it safely to the entrance. Once on the surface, the commander communicated with his base. He was eloquent about his needs. He was assured that reinforcements were on the way.

While the military forces were being augmented, the policewoman went to the house of her chief and roused him from his slumber.

"Chief, in the reservoir are forty or more monsters like the one we killed by the preserve tonight. They killed half a SEAL team and are now devouring them. The rest of us barely escaped. Reinforcements are on the way to Phoenix. I thought you should know."

"Officer Roundel, I'll have your badge for this. You've been insubordinate, criminally so. Who gave you authorization to call in the US military? Do you realize what your actions imply?"

She met his gaze without flinching. "Sir, you ordered me to discover what happened to the four missing fishermen in the reservoir. You said I could use any resources I could muster. You said you wanted me to discover the truth so I discovered the truth. I've relayed my findings to you. My mission is accomplished."

The chief was reddening and his fists were clenched. "I did not want to find THIS truth!"

"Chief, the four fishermen were killed and eaten by monsters of the same species as the one we left dead by the preserve earlier this night. Those fishermen will not return. The SEAL team members who lost their lives tonight likewise will not return. What are your instructions?"

"Give me your badge and gun. You are suspended indefinitely pending review of your actions. If you breathe one word about what you *think* happened below in the reservoir, I'll throw you in solitary confinement."

Officer Roundel handed the chief her emblems of authority.

"What about the safety of the citizens you swore to protect and serve?"

"Officer Roundel, I'm trying to avoid a wholesale panic. I've been called by this state's two senators, all our representatives and the governor. I've assured them all that the danger has been contained and the case has been closed. The image of that reporter cut to pieces by that monster has given a black eye to this state throughout the nation."

"Consider, sir, how things will look when forty monsters start roaming the streets of Phoenix devouring and terrorizing its citizens."

"Young lady, that's all I want to hear from you tonight. I have your badge and gun. You know what you're not to do. Why don't you go home and get some sleep? Perhaps after rest, you'll begin to reason properly."

"Good night chief. It's almost morning. I'm now a free agent. You can keep my badge and gun. I won't need them. Pardon me, but I've still got work to do."

She turned and skipped to the car where the SEAL team commander was waiting for her. "Let's drive," she said.

When she looked back, she saw the chief of

police shaking his fist in her direction. She wondered how long he would last against the forty monsters with a handgun and a badge.

"We can make Sky Harbour in thirty minutes. I need a coffee and a donut. What about you, sailor?"

Two hours later the troop transport landed with three armed personnel carriers. The SEAL commander was glad to see his reinforcements with their powerful armaments. He did not take long to explain what had happened. He outlined the plan of attack. He ordered issuance of arms to the policewoman and told his men that she was part of their team now.

This time the military could not hide from the press corps, who had surrounded Sky Harbour hoping for the right moment to discover the truth. The SEAL commander did not disappoint them. He explained why his men were present and what they intended to do. His rendition was so fierce, no one dared to question him. When his statement was done, he took the lead vehicle and led his troops to the entrance of the reservoir. There like an armada, they launched for the far side of the water.

They found the far landing altered from the time they left it. The campfire had burned out. There was no sign of the bodies of the fallen soldiers. Likewise, there were no monsters visible.

The commander asked the former policewoman, "What do you think?"

"I think we'd better look on the surface in the preserve."

The military retraced their passage and made haste on the surface toward the preserve. There everything appeared calm in the morning light. The grisly sights of the previous night's encounters had been removed. The threat of monsters had vanished in the Arizona sunshine.

A motorcade of mayors and police chiefs arrived as if on cue. The media circus formed a semicircle around the dignitaries. The governor arrived by helicopter as did Arizona's two senators. The banners and signs heralded a great victory of good over evil. A monster had been vanquished, and everyone wanted to take a bow before the cameras.

A band began to play. Buses with citizens arrived to fill out the audience. Speeches began. Everyone had something touching to say about the fallen reporter. No one, it seemed, had stood idly by while the monster was slain. Everyone had taken a part in killing the beast.

The police chief darkly mentioned miscreants who overstepped their authority—by whom he meant the policewoman from whom he had taken the weapon and the badge. He gestured at the military presence, claiming they were present for a routine training exercise and not as participants in the successful law enforcement effort. He made no mention of the gallant men who had died trying to kill the monsters in the reservoir.

The chief's single refrain was that the menace was dead and the people of Phoenix were safe again. He revelled in the applause.

The media played their role to perfection. No nagging questions were raised. The SEAL team commander's speech at Sky Harbour remained unmentioned—it had been effectively squelched by the news editors and all copies of the recordings had been destroyed.

All in all, it was a perfect Arizona day, the orange sunlight cutting through a cloudless light-blue sky.

As the festivities subsided and the feasting began, the dignitaries departed in their sundry vehicles. Everyone was beaming with satisfaction. No hint of unfinished business blemished the occasion. Greater Phoenix did what it did best: it rejoiced with blissful abandon. The military guests were regaled with the rest. Before they took off from Sky Harbour late that afternoon, every man had eaten and drunk his fill.

Commander Curlow shook his head as he shook the former officer Bekkah Roundel's hand goodbye. She wanted to say something, but he raised two fingers to his lips.

"A routine training exercise," he said. "We live to fight another day. I'm sure we'll have another opportunity."

Roundel was crestfallen as she watched the giant military transport lift off. She drove home disconsolate and wondered what she would do now that she had no livelihood.

That evening as she ate a slice of delivered pizza, she received a call.

"You may not remember be—there's no reason you should, but I'm Carrie Anderson. My boyfriend Daniel Strong and I saw the first evidence of the monster by the Riparian Preserve."

"Yes, I recognize your voice from the camcorder recording. It was an inspiration to me throughout the early stages of my quest to get to the bottom of what was happening."

"And did you *really* get to the bottom of what was happening?"

"No, not really. In such cases, you may achieve some measure of success, but people can only stand to dig a little into the mysteries that harbour their inmost fears."

"I've been thinking about the survival of the monsters. I mean, killing one monster can't be the end of the affair. They killed one monster. Then they killed another. Yet monsters have survived for thousands of years. I can't help but think there are thousands of monsters for every one we are lucky enough to kill."

"And your point is, Carrie?"

"My point is simply that I understand what you're up against. The public pronouncements of self-important dignitaries do nothing for me. I want to thank you from the bottom of my heart for being impervious to public opinion."

"And that's why you called me tonight—to

thank me?"

"Yes. I hope you'll continue doing the good, honest work no one else wants to do."

The former policewoman looked at her cellphone long after the call had been terminated. What did Carrie Armstrong really know? Was she aware of the threat that lay waiting in the Black Rock Reservoir? Or was she simply clairvoyant?

A knock on her front door disturbed her thoughts. She opened it to find her chief outside on her porch, with a chagrined look on his face and her badge and gun in his two hands.

"I won't impose on you. I just stopped by to say I was out of line to take your symbols away. I'm restoring them to you and reinstating you to your former status. I hope you'll come back. I need you—the citizens of this city need you."

She took the badge and weapon from the chief and nodded. He saluted her, and she returned his salute.

"Good night, then. I'll look forward to hearing a *post mortem* from you the first thing tomorrow."

"Thank you, sir. I'll be there with my report." She closed her door and locked it.

Back to the door, she ran her finger over her shield. Weighing her pistol in her hand, she put it in her holster. She felt whole again, but a little sad. She mused that the call to duty from Carrie Anderson and her chief's recall notice were entirely coincidental. She wondered whether such intersections in time were significant or only accidental. Maybe they were both.

The best part of her evening was the call she received from the SEAL team commander. He did not say much, only that he was proud—again—to have served with her. "One day, Bekkah, I'll come and take you out to dinner at a nice restaurant—for pleasure, not business."

"I'd like that very much, Lance."

"I know how hard it must have been for things to have turned out as they did today."

"I know how hard it must have been for *you* to lose half your team to monsters."

They were both speechless for a few minutes with their unvoiced, separate thoughts.

"Well, I've got to write a few reports."

"Gosh, Lance, so do I. Thanks for reminding me."

"How long do you think we have?"

"Oh, you mean, 'How long do we have before we have to fight the monsters again?'"

"Yes, that."

"After a feast, there's digestion. I suspect they'll be ready to feed again inside the month."

"I'll plan accordingly."

"That's just as well. Goodbye."

Officer Roundel spent till midnight writing her after-action report. It all boiled down to a single page of bullet statements. Its purpose was not only to document events, but also to warn about the future.

The next morning, she made it to police formation and handed her report to the chief at the special meeting he called in her honour. The meeting began by his reading her report verbatim. When he had finished, he applauded her, and the others in the room followed suit.

"In keeping with the recommendations in your report, I want you and the others here to write an action plan to deal with other such incidents as we have just endured. I want you to think 'blue sky' and without limit. You know the threat better than anyone else. Make your plan worthy of combatting the real threat. Keep your Special Forces friends in the picture. In fact, I've requested the leader of the SEAL team to join you for a few days. Officer Roundel, you have friends in high places. Use them to our mutual advantage."

Commander Curlow arrived late in the afternoon after Roundel had worked her own team to formulate a draft plan. Together in a suite at the Camelback Hilton, she and the commander worked past midnight to refine her plan to include the military point of view.

Lance told her, "The trouble with any plan is our inability to gauge the enemy properly. If we are facing forty monsters, we can assuredly conquer. If we are facing forty-thousand monsters, we may have trouble."

"Let's go with what we know, Lance. We know that somewhere between forty and forty-eight monsters dwell in the reservoir and in the preserve. More may augment their numbers, but we'll have to deal with a surge capability to suit."

"Spoken like a military commander!"

Over a room-service meal, they retooled the plan to accommodate surge. By the time she left for home that night, she felt as if the plan might actually work as designed. Whenever she got cocky, though, she recalled how many brave men had died by underestimating their foes. She doubled down and tweaked her product until she was unsure to the correct degree. Roundel was plagued by the idea that her plan must be executed whenever needed. That might be instantaneously—tonight or tomorrow, perhaps.

"Commander, I'm sorry to bother you after working you so hard this evening. What would it take to keep a SEAL team in garrison in Phoenix continuously from now until we fight?"

"Bekkah, you must have been reading my mind. I've advised Tampa that we'll be on an extended training exercise indefinitely starting tomorrow afternoon."

"Thank you!"

"My pleasure. I hope you can get some deep sleep. You'll need it."

The commander was as good as his word. The next afternoon Sky Harbour was host to three huge cargo planes holding three complete SEAL teams. Meanwhile, as a precaution, all the police forces of Greater Phoenix kept an unobtrusive vigil around the preserve, at the entrance to the reservoir and around all rivers and waterways throughout the city, from the Salt River south to the Gila River. Until she had been forced to consider all the places the monsters might be hiding, Roundel was not aware of how much standing water there was in this desert location.

The SEAL teams populated garrisons in Gilbert, Scottsdale and Phoenix proper. They exercised daily and waited for the opportunity to engage the monsters. The media did not pester the military, but they stood ready to roll out in force to cover any combat actions. Within two weeks, the military and police presence blended into the background—it was the new normal.

Murphy of the infamous Murphy's Laws was present in Greater Phoenix. The first sign of his presence was the haboob that advanced from Tucson in a wall of sand five miles high with lightning and tornadoes. As the storm engulfed Sun Valley, tearing up trees and filling the land with floods, corpses of hundreds of feral cats were seen floating in Oak Tree and Merrill Parks. The animals had been mutilated horribly and skinned before they died. Alert to such evidence, Officer Roundel sounded the alarm—the monsters were feasting in the storm beyond the Riparian Preserve.

Commander Curlow sent one SEAL team to the preserve and another to the reservoir. The third team he held in reserve to reinforce either of the others that had the need.

He personally commanded the team sent to

the preserve. He ordered his men to slay monsters as they entered or departed the preserve. Because of the high water level and the continuing storm, the boundaries of the preserve were unclear. The SEALs were ready to fight the monsters from boats or in the water. Where Greenfield Street was supposed to run, an enormous monster arose from the water to confront the team.

If Grendel was the monster in the poem *Beowulf* and Grendel's mother was the greater foe, so the huge beast that reared in front of Lance Curlow's boat looked like the sire of Grendel's mother. It was not fourteen feet tall, but twenty, and its movements were both subtle and deadly. Five SEALs were cut in half with the monster's first vicious pass.

Curlow stood undaunted. He took his specially sharpened knife between his teeth and dived into the rushing water. He did not evade the sweeps of the monster's webbed appendages but sought them, using his blade to wound the creature and hoping for the beast to bring him close enough to strike home to its heart. The blade hung in the great creature's hand, which drew back swiftly. Curlow was drawn by the action to the place he bargained for.

Loosening his knife, Curlow swam directly toward the monster's chest and used his weapon to open the beast's abdomen. With one hand hooking inside the monster's chest cavity and the other probing inside for the heart, Curlow found his target and sliced the writhing creature's in-nards. In the process, the beast flailed and coursed widely before its vital systems failed. Then it died and lay pouring blood into the water as the SEAL commander sought his troops. A black rubber ves-sel found him and its skipper informed Curlow that other monsters, smaller than the massive one the commander killed, were being pursued throughout the area.

The pitched watery battle continued, with many dozen feats of individual combat, SEALs on monsters, the results uneven in spite of the valour of the combatants. Commander Curlow ordered all slain monsters to be bound together as a float-ing mass, in part to draw other monsters to them.

The tactic worked. Instinctively, other mon-sters gathered where their slain counterparts floated. SEALs picked their targets from those approaching water beasts. Meanwhile, the storm continued with lightning and torrential rain. Never had the SEAL team encountered more for-midable foes. Their glory was compounded by de-feating them.

Finally, another pattern emerged. Officer Roundel received reports from Lance Curlow indi-cating the remaining monsters were making their way to the entrance to the Black Rock Reservoir. The second SEAL team was therefore prepped to engage the monsters returning to the reservoir. It became in hindsight a target-rich environment. Fresh troops combatted monsters fleeing for their lives. Where ordinary weapons failed, SEALs took their knives into the sandy water to fight the monsters mano-a-mano as their commander had done. Brown water thus was stained red with blood.

Curlow's team closed on the entrance to the reservoir, driving scores of monsters before them. The beasts were intercepted by the waiting SEAL team. The entry was a mass of writhing limbs and webbed appendages. Slashing and grappling, the SEALs held sway.

Curlow saw his opportunity and ordered the reserve SEAL team to press toward the reservoir. The enemy monsters were converging to make their last stand. The SEALs needed to act with force immediately and not stint till the job was done. From her vantage, Officer Roundel saw what was happening. Her electronic display indicated the pincers actions of the first and second SEAL teams at the reservoir's entry. The third SEAL team was closing on the area, annihilating all monsters in their path.

As suddenly as the haboob began, it stopped. The afternoon light was resplendent, but the battle still raged. Into the reservoir poured the three SEAL teams, chasing the monsters, whose rage was translated into vicious attacks on all sides. If earlier combat had been defined by individual acts of heroism, now it was group against group. The SEALs surrounded the flailing monsters in the water. Special Forces took revenge for the wanton killings on the shore. No quarter was given to the monsters, and the beasts expected none.

As a monster raised its head above the water, a SEAL jumped to engage it. When a SEAL was finished with one enemy beast, he selected another and killed it also. There was no ambiguity about which were enemy monsters in this fight. All monsters must die. And die they did.

From the entry to the opposite side of the Black Rock Reservoir, the monsters were driven, all three SEAL teams pressing them on all sides. At the far end, the survivors among the monsters crawled ashore, only to be caught in the withering cross-fire from all three SEAL teams. Curlow saw the situation clearly. He ordered two teams to flank the mass of enemy fighters, and he led his own third team into the midst of the fray.

Curlow had trained his men in the sands of Afghanistan, Iraq and Syria. Now that training was used to effect. The monsters had no escape. The SEALs gave them no respite. No SEAL was unengaged. Close-quarters fighting was the order of the day. When a monster decided to make a break for the reservoir, the flanking SEALs cut it down with withering fire.

So the battle continued in the dark for hours. Special Forces soldiers, the best in the world, were faced with an almost-equal adversary. In the end, the monsters lost, but at a terrible cost to the SEALs. Fifteen dead and thirty wounded SEALs attested to the savagery of the fight.

The Sargasso Sea of monsters' bodies was

hauled to the reservoir's entry while the mopping-up operation continued. As helicopters flew the wounded SEALs to medical facilities, logistical support personnel numbed the monster casualties. In total, one-hundred-twenty monsters were slain. By far the largest of the slain was the grandsire monster Lance Curlow had personally slain.

As the waters receded after the Haboob, Officer Roundel found Commander Curlow as he emerged from the reservoir.

"Did you kill all the monsters?"

"We killed all we found. The operation is continuing."

"What should I tell my chief?"

"Tell him, we slew all the monsters we could find. More may have survived, but we'll get them all eventually. Also tell him, his victory came at a terrible cost."

Roundel hugged Curlow in an unprofessional way. He reciprocated until he had to pull back to continue his operation. "Let's remember where we left off hugging so we can continue later."

Officer Bekkah Roundel went to her chief and explained what had happened. He was triumphant, but he counselled silence about the entire operation.

"Your plan worked. We might have faced much worse than the death of a thousand feral cats. Are you sure your SEAL friends will contain the menace?"

"Sir, if anyone on earth can contain the monsters, the SEALs can."

"Well, then. There's no reason to alarm the citizens about what might have been. The media don't need to be informed. Tomorrow will be another normal day in paradise. Right?"

"If you say so, sir. And I suppose the casualties among the SEALs will be chalked up to another training exercise gone horribly wrong."

"Your friends are capable of spinning their own tales, I'm sure. As for you, I'm going to recommend a commendation."

"Please, Chief, nothing for me—except the opportunity to revise my disaster plan to account for Mr. Murphy."

"Mr. Murphy?"

"Yes, sir. Murphy of Murphy's laws. You know: 'If anything can go wrong, it will go wrong, at the worst possible time and with the worst possible consequences.'"

The chief shook his head but said, "As you wish, Officer Roundel. At least accept my personal thanks for having the courage to work for the citizens in spite of the bureaucracy."

"Yes, sir."

The SEAL teams lifted off from Sky Harbour without fanfare one week later. The cargo weights were diminished somewhat, but none of the civilians noticed. That evening, Commander Lance Curlow phoned Officer Bekkah Roundel.

"Hi, Bekkah. Remember I promised to invite

you to dinner on pleasure, not business?"

"How could I forget? Where are you now?"

"When the troops took off, I remained to tie up loose ends and write reports. How about having that dinner tonight?"

"What do you have in mind?"

"I know a steak place in Scottsdale if you're game for dinner tonight."

"You're on, Beowulf!"

"So you've given me a new nickname?"

"You earned it, sailor. By the way, the wine pairing for the steak will be your next important test."

"Do you like Bordeaux wines?"

"I do. And we have a number of things to celebrate, don't we?"

"More than you might expect. I'll text you the time and place. All you need to do is follow your navigation system to the destination. I'll be there."

Bekkah Roundel was busy completing her final reports to wonder what Lance had meant by his comment, "more than you might expect." She finished her work in time to have plenty of time to shower, dress and drive to Scottsdale. When she arrived at the restaurant, Curlow was sitting at their table with two bottles of fine Bordeaux wines already uncorked and breathing.

"Bekkah, you look stunningly beautiful this evening."

She blushed and sat as he manoeuvred her

chair. "You're looking none the worse for wear after killing ten dozen monsters, one with your bare knife."

He smiled and held up two fingers to his lips to indicate silence. "Tonight is pleasure, not business, remember?"

During dinner, Lance took the opportunity to introduce himself as a person, not a SEAL. Still, he cut a fine figure of a naval officer in spite of not wearing a uniform. Bekkah hung on his every word like a schoolgirl on her first date. She too had to tell him as much as she could about herself.

While they were having fun and drinking wine, a bouquet of flowers arrived at their table. It was from the chief of police, together with an attached note that he personally was going to pay for the couple's wine: "You have both done Greater Phoenix a service for which no payment would be sufficient. Therefore, accept as my personal gift the dinner wine you are enjoying."

"Your chief is not entirely a bad person, I think."

"You're probably right, Lance, but you have some explaining to do too."

"I do?"

"You mentioned in your call that we'd be celebrating 'more than I might expect.' So please explain."

"Bekkah, we've done things few other couples have been privileged to accomplish. Do you recall how we put ourselves at risk to lure the first monster from the water so we could kill it?"

"How could I forget?"

"Well, now we've done all that again, only with many monsters."

"And your point is, sailor?"

The handsome naval officer stood up and knelt by her side as he looked into her eyes.

"Bekkah Roundel, I love you and want you to be my wife." He handed her a ring box and waited for her answer.

Bekkah opened the box and admired the fire of the marquise-cut diamond that lay in the setting of the ring. "Oh, Beowulf, this is so sudden. The ring is beautiful. Of course, I'll be your wife. You've made me happy beyond my wildest belief."

He placed the ring on her ring finger and kissed her lightly on the lips. The other patrons of the restaurant applauded as he resumed his seat.

The rare fillet mignons came right on time, and the pairing with the wine was perfect according to the sommelier, who had recommended—successfully—the Chateau Petrus 1972.

The establishment photographer took a picture, which the next morning she sold to the Arizona *Republican.*

The couple were holding hands in the newspaper picture, whose caption read, "Who's Moisting Who's Hand," a tribute to the equality of the match. The diamond ring was flashing in the photo, symbol enough of the relationship between the two young people.

As the next day was a working day for both Lance and Bekkah, they went their separate ways after dinner. Lance said he was going to drive back to his hotel and make preparations for an early morning departure. Bekkah said she was going to drive to the Riparian Preserve to survey the black waters before she went home to bed.

Bekkah walked along the edge of the preserve. A mild wind was blowing, and the stars were twinkling in the clear sky. On the rim of the preserve, Bekkah saw a lump extending into the water. She recalled the image described by Daniel Strong and Carrie Anderson on the police camcorder many weeks prior. She approached the lump unafraid and used her cellphone pen light to examine it closely.

The lump was a fallen palm tree, no doubt stricken by the recent storm. While she observed it, something pulled it into deeper water where it submerged. Bekkah wondered what would have happened if the same phenomenon had been observed by the former couple. She also wondered what might have pulled the tree under the water's surface now. A frisson of fear ran down her spine.

Bekkah shrugged and continued her nocturnal walk and reverie. She was now engaged to be married to a genuine hero with whom she had been involved on many professional levels. She let her mind fly to consider what it would be like to marry the present-day counterpart to the hero

Beowulf. He was clearly bigger than life, as had been the monster he had slain.

She thought of the innocent victims of the monsters—Hazel Groundswell, Hazel's girlfriend Dawn Larsen and the four fishermen. She shivered uncontrollably as her mind touched on each victim. She felt again how good it felt to be rid of the first monster long ago and how unsettling she felt about the return of the creature, only in large numbers. For a moment, she did the math. Were all the monsters destroyed in the SEAL team operations? How could anyone know the truth of that?

Off to the right, Bekkah heard a huge splash. She could not imagine what had caused the sound. Hadn't Daniel and Carrie heard such a splash? Should she be frightened?

She heard footsteps behind her, but when she turned, no one was there. She heard slapping of webbed feet on sidewalk. Was her mind playing tricks on her? She turned to retrace her steps, but she saw a tall figure standing in her path. She was not wearing a side arm. She was entirely defenceless. Was the figure a threat?

"Hello, Bekkah! Don't be frightened. It's only me."

She gasped with relief. "Hi, Lance. You followed me."

"I confess, I did. I wasn't sure what my future bride might be thinking. I should have guessed that you'd come to the place where our latest little adventure began."

"Did you hear the huge splash a moment ago?"

"I did, but I cannot account for it."

"Neither can I. When I arrived, a palm was lying in the water, but it was pulled deeper and sank beneath the surface."

"You're sure it was just a palm?"

"Yes. I used my cell phone's pen light to verify the fact."

"I think it's time for you to be getting home. Do you want me to follow you there?"

"No need. But, yes, I should be getting home. It's been a long day with a nice ending—I mean dinner with your proposal and my acceptance."

"I'm glad we had the chance to make ourselves clear. You've been on my mind since I first met you. When I was fighting the largest monster I ever want to confront, all I could think of was getting back to you."

"Well, here I am."

He took her in his arms and held her close. Then he walked her to her car and watched as she drove off. For a long while he remained next to the preserve, just watching the water.

When he was satisfied no monster was going to emerge to challenge him, he returned to his hotel to complete his preparations for his flight home. Bekkah knew these things because he texted her the next morning before his flight took off. He also texted he would be back to Phoenix soon to help plan their wedding, but first he had to learn Old English to learn the truth about the new nickname she had given him, Beowulf.

THE LAST TRUMP

E. W. Farnsworth

My name is Farrah Linder. I am an internally displaced person, or IDP, in America. I am not alone. Before the End Time, I could connect with friends all over the world. Not now. There is no longer any communication network infrastructure on land, under the sea, in the air or in space. What good are computers and cell phones without networks? What good are friendships and links when no one can help anymore? I hide and watch for the right time to move. I wait for the next opportunity to make it a little farther toward the southern border.

My father told me it would be like this after the bombs rained on Washington, New York, Chicago and Los Angles, Phoenix and St. Louis, all the other major cities, now destroyed. I did not believe him at the time. Dad was right, of course. He left me a precious legacy—a map and instructions, which are folded in my pocket and engraved in my mind. I refused to listen to him while he was still among the living. How I wish he were still with me. Now I have only my own wits to survive. They will have to suffice. In the cold, starless desert with the dense radioactive clouds blocking the moon, I rest under a saguaro while I plan the night.

My father's name is Edward Linder. He will be remembered as the architect of American military response in event of terminal attack. He told me what would happen explicitly—he called it the Single Integrated Operational Plan, the SIOP. The government would keep the attack a secret. No one would be warned. The president and his cabinet would take off in Air Force One and Air Force Two. Congress would evacuate to the mountain enclave in West Virginia.

Those in the Mountain in Colorado would fight the war to the bitter end. But the end would come within forty-five minutes from the first indication of incoming ballistic missiles. We had no defence against such an attack. All we could do was counter attack to assure the end of Moscow and Beijing and hundreds of other enemy cities.

In the ensuing free-for-all, Dad predicted that the Russians would level Europe and the Chinese would level Japan and Korea as well as the Western USA. Conventional forces would remain scattered all over the world, but radioactive fallout in the form of black rain would circle the globe and cause a general extermination of humanity.

Dad saw it all clearly. He said the world had gone quite mad. He explained the outcome in the ancient catch phrase MAD, mutually assured destruction. Dad's eyes bored into mine when he told me that only I and a few others would survive. I knew the rules for what could be foreseen —flee to the Sea of Cortez where a sailboat was waiting for me at our summer place. The boat was stocked with enough food and medical supplies to last a year.

Forty-eight hours before SIOP, Dad phoned me and gave the code word he had drilled into my consciousness: TRUMP. It was our private joke that the biblical "Last Trump" of the book of Revelation was in the name of the man who had ironically become the President. He was not evil precisely, but he came, like Murphy of 'Murphy's Laws," at the worst possible moment in America's chequered history. What followed his inauguration was as much the fault of his feckless opponents and the press as of his fervent, mindless followers. Now it hardly matters who was to blame. Dad told me the woulda-coulda-shoulda people would finally be silenced by the magnitude of the global catastrophe.

I who always mocked my father as a form of youthful rebellion climbed into my Jeep and drove to the Interstate 10. My kit was already packed, so I needed only walk to the garage, push the opener button, slip the key into the ignition and back the car into the street. I passed oblivious drivers speeding north and south, and I wondered at the morality of not raising a general alarm. I had resolved not to do that as no one would believe what I was saying. Would a reasonable person take action on the words of an impressionable seventeen-year-old girl like me? I don't think so. In fact, I believe I would have been arrested as a lunatic. Anyway, if I told the authorities the source of my information, they would have arrested Dad and placed him in one of their many concentration camps.

In Social Studies classes, I had been taught that the counterintelligence state was foremost determined to protect the system it had created out of whole cloth. The moment I broke ranks and fled, I was an enemy of the state. There was no going back. The barriers I had to cross were numerous, and like a rat in a complex maze, I had to follow instructions explicitly, or I would be lost.

I left the highway for dirt roads leading to the border. At an adobe ruin three miles from the Great Wall, I parked the Jeep and covered it with the sand-coloured tarp I had brought for the purpose. I slid under the vehicle and waited, catching sleep while I listened to a small transistor radio for the news. The great blast came before the war was even announced. I pulled on my gas mask and waited. Phoenix, I knew, had been levelled. A hot wave passed over my position. Dad had counselled me to park with the adobe ruin between me and the city. By the infernal light, I saw saguaros outlined like human figures with arms akimbo.

When the radiation wave had passed, I waited a full hour. After that I crawled out from under the Jeep and pulled on my backpack. My cell phone was now worthless. I drew my Colt revolver and used my hand compass to guide me to the small house five hundred feet from the Wall. Its roof had blown off, but under the trapdoor was the mouth of the tunnel. I descended, keeping my gun at the ready. The tunnel led down under the Wall, but I had no idea what I might find in it.

I moved in darkness, hugging the tunnel's smooth wall to my right. Dad had warned me not to turn back but persevere until I reached the other side. I was terrified of the unknown in the darkness, even more than I had been of the heat and radiation from the bomb. I sincerely hoped the usual residents of the little house in Mexico were not waiting for me to emerge through their trapdoor. I reached the other end of the tunnel and listened for noises through the wooden door at the top of the stairs. Hearing nothing, I pushed up the trapdoor and climbed into a roofless barn. No human challenged me. The animals had fled. I did not waste time but walked straight through the desert landscape toward the Sea of Cortez. By my map, I had five locations to use during daylight hours. I would only move at night to avoid detection.

I was glad I was wearing my cowgirl boots because the night was filled with the sound of rattlers rattling. I was also glad I had been trained as a dead shot. I had no fear of handling any single hombre who stood in my path. Four days was my plan to reach the sailboat. I had no provision to meet anyone as a guide or helpmeet. I reached my first stopover at daybreak and hid in the loft of the deserted dwelling. Looking through the wooden slats at the desert, I thought it odd how little changed from my last visit it was. Dad and I had made the trip together to practice what I was now going through. It was prudent of Dad to be so thorough. He had taught me well knowing he would not be with me on this final journey. I slept soundly until I heard the old woman speaking with her son.

The woman was advising her son to ride the family's mule south as far as he could manage. She told him she would follow when she was able. There would be no drugs shipments for a long time. She told him the coyotes would sleep as well. The gringos had done the worst of things. She doubted anyone was alive north of the Wall. The boy rode off on the mule. The woman shook her head and rummaged through the building below where I was hiding. I did not reveal myself to her. She went about her business of gathering a few belongings. Then she walked slowly in a southerly direction. I fell asleep again, hoping to awaken after sunset for the next leg of my journey.

I was startled by a boisterous argument of a group of four or five hard men, who had settled below in the dwelling for the night. I listened for news, but the men were focused on their plans to forge north under the Wall to reconnoitre. What with the devastation, they figured they would have the pick of the leavings. They discounted the radioactivity. Their leader boasted that they would find gold and silver aplenty. Maybe, he said, they would find women desperate for company. At this they all laughed wickedly. I felt my gun for reassurance.

When the men had fallen asleep, I crept down from the loft and continued on my way. That the men had not posted a guard indicated they did not feel threatened on the Mexican side of the Wall. I was aware that dozens of tunnels extended into America from Mexico. Perhaps, I thought, many other opportunists would do as those men planned to do. I was moving against the inevitable tide streaming north. Who else would be walking to the Sea?

My second stopover was an adobe hut on what might have been a small farm once. I did not stay on the floor of the one-storey building. Instead, I climbed to the roof and positioned myself below the place where the façade rose above the flat cover. I was taking a risk that no aerial surveillance would be employed while I was waiting for nightfall. As it happened, the air vehicles were concentrated to the north along the Wall. What did the Mexican authorities care about a sleeping figure on a rooftop twenty miles below the border? I slept under my brown serape and sombrero, careful to search the place where I lay for brown scorpions before I lay down. As the sun rose, the rattlers' music filled the air. I slept in fits and starts all day. When I climbed down after sunset, I resolved to walk all the way to the seacoast, risking daylight contact in the process.

That night I overtook Jose and his mule. I avoided contact and pressed along the highway, ducking behind cover when I saw lights or heard motor vehicles approaching. I saw the pink eyes of jackrabbits dotting the darkness as headlights passed. I gave a group of women and children a wide berth. They were heading toward the coast, but they would stop for the night for the children's sake. I heard the women talk about a plan for the Army to seal the Wall against the possibility that the gringos would want to come south. One old senora laughed as she opined that the tables had now turned on the North Americans. I bristled at her hatred. I knew she would show me no mercy if she found me invading her country.

I kept walking after daylight as I had planned. I was exhausted, but I kept putting one foot ahead of the other. I was now running low on water. In Arizona, I always kept two full bottles on my person wherever I went. Now I was down to my last two bottles, and I had to ration my use of water strictly. I also had to find replenishment of that precious liquid. I knew the heat would rise throughout the day. It would be hottest at evening. Then the night would cool off. I would make the seacoast the following day at noon.

I had been so focused on following my plan that I had not dwelled on the destruction the senseless bombing had caused around the world. Hundreds of millions were dead. A way of life was now obliterated. The mighty American Empire had been brought low. I was trespassing in Mexico for my own survival. I feared being discovered and robbed—or worse. I had no idea what I was going to do once I boarded my sailboat. I had a frisson of fear that someone might have absconded with the boat anyway.

I was lucky to have missed being accosted. A woman, particularly a blonde gringo, traveling alone might be a good target for malice or lust. I did not want to use my pistol as that would certainly bring the law to bear. Prayer works. I made it to the Sea of Cortez. My sailboat was moored to the pier where Dad had tethered it. Raoul, the man we paid to keep it ship shape was scrubbing the decks when I arrived. He waved at me kindly. He knew why I had come.

"Senorita Linder," Raoul said, "I'm glad you made it. The boat is ready. It has everything aboard as your father planned. I have a request, though."

"Raoul, what do you need? If it is in my power, I'll satisfy you."

"My wife and son would like to go with you. I would too. If we all travel together, we'll be safer than if you go alone."

"How soon can your family be ready, Raoul?"

"I will fetch them within the hour. You sail out into the sea and come back in when you see us on the pier."

I nodded and added, "Raoul, be quick. If you aren't back by nightfall, I might have to sail without you." I knew that a Mexican hour might stretch into many days. This was Mañanaland, after all.

Raoul looked sick until I stuck up my thumb and smiled. He took heart and raced to fetch his family. Meanwhile, I cast off the lines and sailed offshore. I tacked back and forth for three hours as the sun gradually set. I saw Raoul waving from the pier, but he was alone. I closed on the pier. He jumped into the boat and pushed off.

"We have to meet Rosa and Pablo down the shore a mile. The policia are searching for gringos with the intent to inter everyone they find. You go below decks. I'll swing the boat toward shore and pick up my family. We'll get away if we're agile."

I had to trust Raoul. I had no other choice. I crawled below decks and waited as he swung toward shore and picked up his wife and son. As he swung out into the sea, a police car with its siren blaring pulled up onto the beach. The officers drew their weapons, but Raoul had steered straight out into the sea. He pretended he did not hear the calls from the police officer's bullhorns. They fired their guns into the air. Raoul was stead-fast. Rosa waved at the shore, her other hand on her son's shoulder.

The policemen shrugged and returned to their car. Raoul laughed. Then he asked me to come up to the weather deck.

"Senorita, we have fresh tortillas and refried beans for dinner. I'll steer while you feast with my family. We must keep sailing out to the centre of the sea lest the police send a boat to search us. Meanwhile, we're going to have to plan our journey wisely."

I was, again, lucky to have Raoul. As we sailed, we ate and talked until late in the night. We decided to sail first for Cabo and then south from there to follow the west coast of the continent. We had no idea what we would find along the way or what dangers might await Americans in a world that resented the former might of the United States. I realized I had survived the initial flight, just as my father had planned. Now I had to find a life with none of the preconceptions I had been born with. It was daunting, I thought, but exciting too. There would be life after Trump, but it would certainly not be anything like the one I had figured as my birthright.

INVOCATION TO KEK

Elizabeth Davis

(This invocation was taken from *An Egyptian Handbook of Ritual Power*, a tome similar to the *A Coptic Handbook of Ritual Power*. A small parchment manuscript, 20 pages in length, covered in invocations, drawings, and words of power. However, there are several differences between these two texts. Despite the shared language of Coptic, Hermopolis dialect, the *An Egyptian Handbook of Ritual Power* does not contain references to Baktiotha and Seth, third son of Adam which were a major part of *A Coptic Handbook of Ritual Power*. *An Egyptian Handbook of Ritual Power* instead focuses on the mythology of Ancient Egyptians, making the researchers suspect that these are translations of an older text or perhaps recorded from oral history. Either way, the original source is currently lost to us. Another difference is the practical concerns of exorcising evil spirits, and curing black jaundice in *A Coptic Handbook of Ritual Power*, versus the more esoteric concerns of The *Egyptian*

Handbook of Ritual Power. The final major difference is that instead of parchment, the *Egyptian Handbook of Ritual Power* is bound with covers of leather, something that was not commonly done at the time. The source of these leather is still be identified.)

> Kek, listen to Me!
> I call upon you
> Of the Eight-Fold Ancient Ones
> Of the Serpent-Headed Women
> Of the Frog-Headed Men
> Each opposed, Each balanced, Each joined
> Nu and Nut
> Sky and Sea
> The timeless Water that brings life
> Ḥeḥu and Ḥeḥut
> North and South Atmosphere
> The unbounded Space that allows us to stand tall
> Kekui and Kekuit
> Dark and Light
> The War that measures our time
> Qerḥ and Qerḥet
> Repose and Action
> The Uncommendable Force that grants us motion and release
> Of this Eight-Fold, The Lords of Hermopolis, the city that borders between two Pharaohs
> I call on only one
> Kek, Listen to Me!

I call you Kekui and Kekuit
Descending Darkness and Ascending Light
I call you Ka and Kait
When You and Your sister hold our Vital Spark
She that Releases and You that Smothers
As You hold back Khepri, the scarab who rolls the morning sun
She wears Ra's mantle, the falcon-eye bearer of the noon
I call you Kek and Kauket
Simplified for those left behind
By the one who destroyed Tyre and built Alexandria
Before crossing the sea into lands beyond the eye of Horus
Where his Ka burned him inside out and Ba flew his reach
Of You and Her, I call only You
I do not call the Light
I do not call the Sun
I break the pair-bond
I break the balance
I call only to You
Kek, Listen to Me!
Here I stand,
On the Night where Nut's light—The stars that dictate our destiny—has been snuffed
On the Night where Khonsu's chariot—the fading and growing moon—has entirely left our sky

Here I stand,
Away from the embers of household fires
Away from the torches of the night guard
Away from the lamps of unresting scholars
Here I stand,
I stand in the home of the jackal and vulture
Far from the crocodile croak and hippo roar
Upon these rocks, blessed by your hand, worn smooth by those before me
I continue an unending chain of devotion
Here I stand,
I wear no kilt or shirt
I let Your darkness embrace me like a lover
I wear no wig or headdress
I let Your cold crown me
I wear no sandals,
I let your hunger draw blood
I wear no jewellery
I praise no Gods over You and beg none to spare me Your wrath
I wear no makeup
You don't use eyes to recognize Your own
Kek, listen to Me!
I have brought you an offering to show my power and worth
With my knife, I have spilled blood on these rocks
I have sent their Ka and Ba flying over the darkened Horizon
I will leave their Bodies to rot in Wilderness
I will leave their Names to fade away in the

sand
I will leave their Shadows, their reflection of your darkness, to return to you
Kek, listen to Me!
I ask for Your Darkness
Your Sister's Light is unbearable
I ask for Your Darkness
Your Sister's Light reveals me to neighbours, priests, and rulers
I ask for Your darkness
Your Sister's Light is too harsh, I wilt like drought fields under her watch
I ask for Your Darkness
To protect me as I work, as I rest, as I call Your praises that others fail to hear
I ask for Your darkness
To remember the promise of this world returned to you
Of the sun swallowed
Of the moon swallowed
Of the stars swallowed
Of the fire swallowed
Of the lightening of storms swallowed
Kek, Listen to Me!

Elizabeth Davis is a second generation writer living in Dayton, Ohio. She lives there with her husband and two cats—neither of which have been lost to ravenous corn mazes or sleeping serpent gods. When she's not driving all over the state, she is creating beautiful nightmares and bizarre adventures.

www.ingramcontent.com/pod-product-compliance
Lightning Source LLC
Chambersburg PA
CBHW051952150726
47999CB00004B/1358